NATHAN WOLFE

WOLFE BROTHER'S SERIES, BOOK TWO

SANDI LYNN

SANDI LYNN ROMANCE, LLC

NATHAN WOLFE

(WOLFE BROTHER'S SERIES, BOOK TWO)

New York Times, USA Today & Wall Street Journal
Bestselling Author
Sandi Lynn

Nathan Wolfe

Copyright © 2020 Sandi Lynn Romance, LLC

All rights reserved. No part of this publication may be reproduced, distributed, or transmitted in any form or by any means, including photocopying, recording, or other electronic or mechanical methods without the prior written permission of the publisher.
This is a work of fiction. Names, characters, places and incidents are the products of the authors imagination or are used fictitiously. Any resemblance to actual events, locales, or persons, living or dead, is entirely coincidental.

Cover Photo by Wander Aguiar
Model: Florian

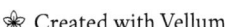 Created with Vellum

MISSION STATEMENT

Sandi Lynn Romance

Providing readers with romance novels that will whisk them away to another world and from the daily grind of life – one book at a time.

CHAPTER 1

*N*athan

"You are one of a kind, Nathan Wolfe." Rebecca's smile grew wide as I climbed out of bed. "I wish you were staying another day."

"Sorry, love, no can do. I have a plane to fly."

"I know. But a girl can hope, can't she?"

I slipped into my clothes and grabbed my watch and wallet from the nightstand.

"Thanks for keeping me company the past couple of days. It was fun."

"It's always fun when you pass through. When do you think you'll be back?"

"I don't know. Probably a month or two. I have to go, or I'll be late."

I leaned over the bed and kissed her lips.

"I'll shoot you a text when the next trip comes up."

"I'll be here, wet and ready." She smirked.

"Damn, Rebecca." I inhaled a sharp breath.

I left her house and climbed into the back of the cab that was waiting outside. Rebecca was one of my regulars that I saw when I flew to Rio de Janeiro. It was always a two-day layover. Just enough time for some casual fun and then a casual goodbye. Just the way I liked it. She was sexy with her long black hair, deep brown eyes and sun kissed skin. The only thing between us was purely physical.

I wasn't any different from my brothers. We all had our issues in one way or another. But then Elijah met Aspen, and as much as he tried to deny his feelings for her, he couldn't. Then they had Mila. I loved my niece to pieces, but I was happy she was just my niece. I could play the role of an adoring uncle, but a father, hell no. Kids weren't my thing, and neither were relationships. Elijah warned me it would happen to me someday and I laughed in his face. I was much stronger in the emotional department than my brother was.

I had the perfect life jetting around the world doing a job I loved and meeting a variety of beautiful women. Women who would do anything for one night with me. I had a gift. The gift of charm and good looks. I could charm the panties off women just by staring into their eyes. I didn't even have to touch them, and they'd be taking off their sexy panties and getting down on their knees to please me. The thing I loved the most about being a pilot was the fact that I was never in one place too long.

***

I stepped off the plane, said goodbye to my crew and headed out of the airport to go home.

"Hey, douchebag!" I heard a voice from behind.

Turning around, I smiled when I saw my brother, Mason, standing there.

"What the fuck are you doing here?" I gave him a bro hug.

"Just thought I'd do my brotherly duty and take you home. Our cab is waiting at the curb. How was Rio?"

"It was fun. No complaints."

"And how is Lucy?"

"You mean Rebecca?" I arched my brow. "Lucy is Spain."

"Sorry, bro. I can't keep all your women around the world straight."

"Rebecca is good. We spent the couple of days I had there in bed." A smirk crossed my lips.

"What are you going to do if Rebecca meets someone?"

"She won't. She's as much as a relationship phobe as I am."

"And if you meet someone?"

"Ha. Do you not know me, little brother? How dare those words even escape your lips."

"I'm just messing with you." He hooked his arm around me.

We took the cab to my apartment, and as we stepped into the elevator, a little girl yelled at us to hold the doors.

"Thank you." She grinned.

"No problem. Which floor?"

"Twenty-two, please."

"Are you visiting someone?" I asked. "I've never seen you around."

"Me and my mom just moved in a few days ago. Do you know everyone that lives in this building?" Her little eye narrowed at me and Mason snickered.

"Actually, I do." My brow raised.

"That's impossible."

"No, it's not, kid."

"Yes, it is. There are thirty-four floors and two hundred and forty-four units in this building. You do not know every single person that lives here. You're lying."

"I don't lie." I cocked my head at her. "How old are you?"

"Nine. How old are you?"

"Thirty-One. You have a few years yet before that smart mouth sets in."

"I guess it hit me early." She smiled.

The doors opened and as she began to walk out, she stopped and turned to me. "If you know everyone that lives in this building, then make me a list. But I know you won't because you're lying and lying isn't nice." She walked away.

"What the fuck?" I looked over at Mason.

"I guess she told you." He laughed as the elevator doors closed.

"You know what? I'm going to prove that little brat wrong."

"Seriously? You're letting a nine-year-old get to you?" He continued laughing.

"She called me a liar."

"She's nine, Nathan. Let it go."

CHAPTER 2

Allison

I inhaled a deep breath and looked around my twelve hundred square foot apartment with the waterline park view. I knew in my heart moving back to New York was the best thing for me and Ruby, even though I hated uprooting her again. The first seven years of her life were spent living in New York before we moved to Chicago. But this is where we belonged. Back home where my family was.

I heard the door open and when I glanced over, I saw Ruby walk inside.

"Where's Grandma?" I asked.

"She's outside talking to a friend of hers. I didn't want to wait so I came up by myself. I'm going to my room to read a book."

"Okay. I'll call you when dinner is ready."

I turned my attention to the stove, stirred the sauce and took a slight taste. Grabbing the garlic salt, I added a little more.

"You'll never believe who I ran into on the street," my mother said as she stepped into the apartment.

"Who?"

"Cora Kline. She finally left that scum of a man she called her husband."

"How long were they married?"

"Thirty years, and he stayed faithful for about five of them. Where's my granddaughter?"

"She's in her room reading. Dinner will be ready in a few minutes. Are you staying?"

"I'd love to, darling, but your father and I are meeting the Patterson's at Daniel. In fact, I need to get home and freshen up. Ruby, come give Grandma a kiss."

She ran from her room and into the arms of her grandmother.

"Bye, Grandma."

"Goodbye, sweetheart. I'll see you tomorrow afternoon." She squeezed Ruby's lips and gave her a kiss. "I'll pick Ruby up tomorrow before you head to the airport."

"That's okay, Mom. I can drop her off."

"No need, darling. We're having lunch with your brother and it's on the way." She kissed my cheek.

She walked out the door, and I set dinner on the table.

"Why do you have to go back to Chicago?" Ruby asked as she took some pasta from the bowl.

"I'm doing it for a client, sweetie. I made a promise that I would still be her lawyer until her case is over. But after this trip, I won't have to go back."

"But if court isn't for two days, why do you have to leave tomorrow?"

"Because I have to be in court early on Wednesday morning and I wouldn't make it in time if I flew out on Wednesday."

"Oh. I get it." She smiled.

"I'll be back Wednesday night. But in the meantime, you're going to have so much fun with Grandma, Grandpa, and Uncle Rick."

It was pouring down rain when I stepped out of the cab with my carry-on and entered through the doors of the JFK airport. Once I made it through security, I headed straight to my gate for my flight was scheduled to leave in an hour. I was looking down at my phone, not paying attention, when suddenly, I ran smack dab into someone.

"Oh my gosh, I'm—" The words stopped flowing from my mouth and I was rendered speechless when I looked up.

"No need to apologize. I wasn't paying attention to where I was walking either." The ungodly sexy man standing mere inches from me grinned as he held up his phone.

My lips formed a smile, and a ding from my phone interrupted our exchange.

"Shit."

"What's wrong?"

"My flight to Chicago is delayed two hours. Ugh."

"So is my flight. Weather conditions. Since we're both delayed how about grabbing something to eat? It'll make the two hours go by faster." A smirk crossed his lips.

I could feel the heat rise in my cheeks as I looked down.

"I already ate. Again, I'm sorry for not paying attention to where I was going. Have a safe flight."

I quickly walked away as I tightly clutched the strap to my carry-on. Wow. I tried my best not to stare at him, but when someone looked like he did, it was hard not to. Six foot two, lean but built body, and alluring green eyes with specks of gold. He sported a light mustache which blended perfectly with the five o'clock shadow that framed his masculine jawline. His hair was a mix of brown and blond, cut short on the sides with a medium length top that was swept up into wispy pieces. To complete his package was his smile. His teeth were beautifully white and perfectly straight. He was definitely a man who took great pride in the way he looked.

I lied to him because I hadn't eaten, and I was hungry. My intention was to grab something before heading to the airport, but time wasn't on my side. It looked like now I had all the time in the world, but I wasn't about to have lunch with that man. As hot as he was, my heart belonged to someone else.

Tears formed in my eyes as I stood across from The Palm Bar & Grille and memories flooded my mind. Memories of when Jared and I ate there together when our flight to Maine was delayed. We went to visit his parents the summer I found out I was pregnant. They had a cottage on the water where they spent most of the summer. I inhaled a deep breath and stepped inside, taking a seat at a small table for two next to the window.

"What can I get for you, darling?" The waitress with the name tag that read "Val" asked.

"I'll have the grilled chicken and avocado sandwich and an order of waffle fries."

"Excellent. I'll put that in for you. Do you want anything else to drink besides water?"

"No. Thank you. Water is fine."

She gave me a smile, grabbed my menu and walked away. Looking around the space, I recalled the day me and Jared sat here. We talked about our plans and our future now that I was pregnant. It was a shock to both of us, and thanks to one college drunken night and one missed birth control pill, Ruby was conceived. We were both nineteen. We had already told my parents and needless to say, they were disappointed, but fully supported us. Jared's parents didn't take it so well. They yelled and spoke of how disappointed they were in both of us for letting it happen. They told me my life was over and I could kiss my education goodbye. But not Jared. They would make sure he finished college and went to medical school exactly how *they* planned. Jared and his parents got into a huge fight that night. We left and got on the next flight back to New York. The first time he'd spoken to his parents since that night was the day Ruby was born. Once they saw her and held her in their arms, they changed their attitude and supported us every way they could.

CHAPTER 3

*N*athan

    The moment she looked up at me with her emerald green eyes, I was done for. Totally in awe of this woman I ran into. She was gorgeous. Drop dead sexy if you wanted my honest opinion. She stood about five foot six with a body that I would kill to explore. It was the way her white skinny jeans clung to her lower half paired with a V-neck embellished pink tank top and white heeled sandals that showed off her perfectly manicured and painted toes. Her long wavy hair was brown with sun kissed blonde highlights. She was perfect and flying to Chicago. My bad mood about being called in to fly the plane on my day off suddenly changed. I had two hours to get to know her better before we took off. The question I had was did she live in New York or Chicago? Either way, no big deal. I'd be seeing her again one way or another.

    I was sleeping when my phone rang, and they asked me to come to work. Technically, they shouldn't have called me because I'd just gotten back from Rio the day before and I had the next two weeks off. But who was I to turn down double time? Plus, it was a quick trip. A little less than three hours each way. But due to the storms that were happening around the country, flights were being delayed all over the place.

One of my favorite places to eat at JFK was The Palm Bar & Grille. They had the best grilled chicken and avocado sandwich and their waffle fries were to die for. Walking to the entrance of restaurant, I spotted the sexy woman I ran into sitting at a table by the window. Hmm. She'd turned me down on my lunch offer because she said she'd already eaten, but yet here she was shoving a waffle fry in her mouth. I casually walked over to her table.

"I see you decided to grab something after all."

She glanced up at me and the color drained from her face.

"Hey," she nervously spoke. "Yeah. I did decide to grab something. Sorry. It's just—"

"No worries. Now that I'm here we can eat together." I grinned as I pulled out the chair across from her and sat down.

"Listen. You seem like a nice guy, but I don't eat with strangers."

"Then let's not be strangers." I extended my hand. "I'm Nathan."

She stared at me for a moment and then hesitantly placed her hand in mine.

"Allison."

"Look at that, Allison. We're no longer strangers." My lip curled.

"Hey you, handsome devil. The usual?"

"Hi Val. Yes, the usual, and I'll just stick with water."

"Coming right up."

"The usual? I take it you dine here often?"

"I do. I travel a lot. How's that grilled chicken and avocado sandwich?"

"It's great. I've eaten here once before and I remembered how good it was."

"And the waffle fries?" I asked.

"Lightly seasoned and cooked to perfection."

"With just the right amount of crisp," we both spoke at the same exact time.

Allison cocked her head and laughed. "Exactly."

"Here you go, Nathan." Val set my plate down in front of me. "Enjoy."

"You know I always do, Val." I gave her a wink.

"That's your usual?" Allison pointed.

"It is. It's obvious we have something in common." The corners of my mouth curved upward.

She looked down and picked up a waffle fry.

"So, why are you traveling to Chicago if you don't mind me asking?"

"Business."

"I take it you're from here."

"I just moved back. I was in Chicago for two years."

She reached in her purse and pulled out her wallet.

"Listen, I really need to go."

"Already? Why don't you stay until I finish, and I'll walk you to your gate?"

"I can't. I need to go make a phone call."

She pulled out her credit card.

"Your meal is on me. It's the least I could do for bumping into you."

"Thanks, but I got it."

"Well, I'm sorry to tell you that it's already been taken care of. I told Val when I walked in to put it on my tab."

"Nathan, please. You don't need to do that."

"I know I don't need to. I want to."

"Thank you. That's really nice of you. I need to get going and make that phone call. It was nice to meet you, Nathan."

"The pleasure was all mine, Allison. I'm sure we'll be seeing each other again."

"Probably not," she spoke as she nervously walked out.

I sat there and pondered the fact that I made her nervous, which was odd because I didn't make women nervous. In fact, I had a hard time getting away from them. But she couldn't escape my presence fast enough. I finished my lunch and headed to the pilot's lounge to change into my uniform.

CHAPTER 4

Allison

Thank God my flight wasn't delayed any longer. I scanned my boarding pass, boarded the plane and took my seat. It would be around ten o'clock when I arrived in Chicago. As I stared out the window at the rain that continued to fall, my mind wandered to thoughts about Nathan. Thoughts about where he was traveling to and if he was also sitting on his flight waiting to take off. I could still smell the scent of him. Clean and fresh with a hint of spice. Not overpowering and not too weak. Just the perfect amount to drive a woman crazy. When I placed my hand in his, I felt a rush of something. An all too familiar feel. Thank God I'd never see him again. The flight attendant walked from seat to seat alerting everyone to fasten their seatbelts as we prepared for takeoff. I reached down in my carry-on and pulled out the case file for tomorrow. As I was looking over my notes, the overhead came on and the pilot started speaking.

"Good evening, ladies and gentlemen. This is Nathan, your captain speaking."

My head whipped up as I listened.

"Welcome to flight 2654 with service to the amazing city of Chicago. I apologize for the delay, but mother nature is in a bad mood today. I know some of you might be nervous fliers as it is, and this weather is only heightening your fear. So I want everyone to take in three deep cleansing breaths before we take off. One. Inhale. Exhale. Two. Inhale. Exhale. Three. Inhale. Exhale. I don't want you to worry. You're in excellent hands with me and I will personally make sure you all arrive to Chicago safe and sound. Now sit back, relax, and enjoy the flight."

"Excuse me?" I signaled for the flight attendant.

"What can I do for you?"

"The pilot. Is he about six two, brownish blond hair, green eyes and has a great smile?"

"Yes." She grinned. "The hottest pilot around as far as I'm concerned. "Do you know him?"

"I ran into him at the airport. He didn't tell me he was a pilot."

"Not surprised. He can be kind of mysterious when he wants to be. Too bad he doesn't mess around with flight attendants. I even considered changing careers just to hookup with him." She gave me a wink.

I casually smiled at her and she walked away and took her seat as the plane began to head down the runway. He knew I was on this flight and yet neglected to tell me he was the pilot. Who does that? And why? He bought me lunch for fuck's sake, and he couldn't be bothered to tell me who he was. Before I knew it, the plane was up in the air and as hard as I tried to concentrate on the case for tomorrow, I couldn't. I found myself irritated by him. *What an asshole.*

"Hello. This Captain Nathan again welcoming you to the rainy but beautiful city of Chicago. We'll be landing soon, so everyone needs to fasten their seatbelts. I can promise you that you won't even feel a thing. My landings are as smooth as they come. I hope you enjoyed the flight. Have a good night everyone."

I rolled my eyes, closed the file folder and stuck it in my carry-on. I was tired and I just wanted to get to my hotel. As soon as the plane landed, we all stood from our seats and waited our turn to exit the plane. I was almost off. So close, and then I saw Nathan standing next to one of the flight attendants with a smile on his face as he stared at me up the aisle. When I approached him, his grin grew wider.

"I told you we'd probably see each other again. Did you enjoy the flight?"

I shot him a look and walked off the plane.

"Allison, wait!"

"Goodbye, Nathan." I scurried from the passenger bridge into the airport.

"At least let me take you to your hotel or wherever you're staying. I have about three hours before I fly back to New York."

I stopped dead in my tracks with my fingers wrapped tightly around the strap of my carry-on and faced him.

"Seriously? Does my face not tell you that I want nothing to do with you?"

"Impossible." He smirked.

"Possible! First of all, I don't even know you and second of all, you failed to mention that you were the pilot on my flight. You knew damn well I was going to be on that plane." I jammed my finger into his chest.

Damn if he didn't look sexy as fuck in his uniform.

"I'm sorry. I should have mentioned it."

"Should've. Would've. Could've. But you didn't. You could have told me when I told you my flight was delayed. But instead you said yours was too. And you could have told me in the restaurant when I specifically asked you if you dined there often and all you said was you travel a lot. Whatever game you're playing is one I'm not interested in. Goodbye, Nathan." I walked away.

"Whatever, Allison. You really need to check yourself." I heard him shout.

Suddenly, I stopped and turned around. I should have kept walking, but he pissed me off and I'd already had a long day and I was tired and agitated.

"By the way, the flight sucked!"

I turned on my heels and headed out of the airport.

CHAPTER 5

Nathan

How dare she? What a psychopath. Thank God I dodged that bullet. Shaking my head, I headed to the pilot's lounge to sit down and relax before I had to fly back to New York. I was tired and pissed off. Why did she have to be so damn sexy even when she was angry? I sighed as I set my alarm so I could sleep for an hour.

I flew back, and the moment my head hit the pillow in my comfy king size bed, I was out. Out for the next twelve hours. When I awoke, I grabbed my phone from the nightstand and saw that I had five text messages from my mother.

"Don't forget family dinner is tonight at seven o'clock."

"Hello? A response would be nice."

"Nathan, are you okay?"

"You didn't crash a plane, did you?"

"I checked the news and there are no crashes, but I'm still concerned why you haven't responded. I'm sending your brother over to check on you."

The last text message came through about five minutes ago. Sighing, I messaged her back.

"Mom. I'm fine. I was sleeping. I had to work last night and I'm tired. I'll be there for dinner. Stop worrying so much.

"I'll never stop worrying about you boys. I'll see you later."

I had just climbed out of bed when there was a knock at the door. It had to be Mason because Elijah was at work.

"You're alive." Mason snickered as I opened the door. "I tried to tell her you were probably sleeping but she insisted I check in on you."

Rolling my eyes, I headed to the kitchen and made a cup of coffee.

"Want some coffee?" I asked.

"Nah. I'm good. What's going on? Why are you just getting up? Is someone in the bedroom?"

"No. I had to fly to and from Chicago last night and I didn't get back until four a.m."

"Why?" I thought you had the next two weeks off."

"I do." I brought the cup up to my lips. "They were down a pilot and asked me to do a quick trip to Chicago. Now I'm off for the next two weeks."

"And I'm off for the next two days. I met this girl last night."

"So did I." I rolled my eyes. "You first."

"Her name is Ashley and she's hot as fuck. I'm meeting up with her for a drink after dinner tonight."

"Is she stable?"

"I'm not sure yet." He laughed. "I'll let you know."

"I met this girl last night in the airport." I finished off my coffee and set the cup in the sink. Turning around, I leaned up against the counter and folded my arms.

"And?"

"She was fucking hot. But she's a psychopath so I'm just going to pretend we never met."

"Why is she a psychopath? What did she do?"

"Laid into me about not telling her that I was the pilot of her flight. You should have heard her ranting and raving while jamming her finger into my chest. Jesus. Then she told me she wasn't interested in whatever game I was playing."

He sat on the stool at the island and let out a loud laugh. "What game were you playing, brother?"

"I wasn't playing anything. She was sexy as fuck and I thought maybe we could have a little fun. Of course I didn't suggest that, but I was silently hoping. I even bought her fucking lunch at The Palm Bar & Grille."

"Did you know she was on your flight?"

"Yeah."

"Then why wouldn't you tell her?"

I shrugged. "I don't know. It never came up, I guess."

"Because you were playing games." He pointed at me. "We can talk about this later. I have to go. I have a few errands to run before heading over to Mom's. Try not to stress over that chick. She's not worth it. You can have any woman you want." He got up and left the apartment.

That wasn't the problem. I specifically wanted her.

※

When I entered my mother's townhome, all I heard was Mila screaming at the top of her lungs. Walking into the kitchen, I found Elijah holding her and trying to calm her down.

"What the hell is going on in here?"

"I don't know what's wrong with her," Elijah spoke.

"I told you, darling, she's teething," my mother said.

"Where's Aspen?"

"Still in court. She'll be here as soon as she gets out."

I walked over to him and grabbed my six-month-old niece from his arms.

"Come to your Uncle Nathan."

She stared at me and instantly stopped crying.

"See. Even babies know how charming I am." I smiled at her. "Unlike some people."

I took Mila with me into the living room, grabbed her plastic keys from the blanket on the floor and handed them to her.

"You think I'm charming, right?"

"What's going on with you?" Elijah asked as he stepped into the room.

"He got cussed out by some chick at the airport he wanted to bang last night. She told him she wasn't interested in whatever game he was playing." Mason laughed as he walked in.

"What?" Elijah laughed. "Some chick turned you down. Impossible." Elijah smirked.

"Right? That's what I said, and she told me it was possible. Doesn't matter anyway, the girl was a total psycho."

I handed Mila over to Mason and she started screaming.

"Take her back. Crying babies make me nervous," Mason spoke as he handed her over to me.

Instantly, she stopped crying.

"How are the wedding plans coming along?" I asked Elijah.

"Good. Did you and Mason get fitted for your tux yet?"

"Shit."

"Language in front of Mila." Elijah pointed at me.

"I mean shoot. I haven't. Have you?" I glanced over at Mason.

"I was going to ask if you wanted to go together tomorrow," he said.

"Sure. What time?"

"I'll let you know tomorrow. Not sure if I'll be able to make it early. Depends on my date tonight." Mason smirked.

"Speaking of—we have a bachelor party coming up." I hooked my free arm around Elijah with a wide grin.

&.

Vincent, the doorman at my apartment building, tipped his hat as he held the door open for me.

"Good evening, Nathan."

"Good evening, Vincent."

I pushed the button to the elevator and patiently waited for it to come down.

"Hello." I heard a child's voice beside me.

Looking down, I saw it was that child from the other day. The one with the smart mouth.

"It's you again. Where are you coming from? Shouldn't you be in bed? It's nine o'clock."

"The playroom just closed and I'm going back up to my apartment. It's summer and I don't have school, so I don't have to be in bed at nine."

"And your mother knows you're down here so late?" I glared at her.

"Yes. Miss Leslie is going to take me up."

"And where is Miss Leslie?"

"Over there." She pointed to where Vincent was standing. "You have that list yet?" she asked as she narrowed her little eye at me.

"Not yet. I'll get it to you. Don't worry."

The elevator doors opened, and Leslie walked over and took the child by the hand.

"Hi Nathan." She smiled as she bit down on her bottom lip.

"Good evening, Leslie."

The elevator stopped on the twenty-second floor. When the doors opened, Leslie and the little girl walked out. She stopped and turned to me before the doors shut.

"I want that list."

"Don't worry. You'll get your list, kid."

The doors shut and I rolled my eyes. But there was something about that kid that made a smile cross my lips.

CHAPTER 6

Allison

I stood in front of my full-length mirror and took one last look at myself, making sure my black pant suit was on point. I had an interview at ten o'clock and I was nervous as hell. Wolfe & Associates was one of the best and largest law firms in New York. They were the firm my father used for his company. He was in a meeting with Caitlin Wolfe, the owner of the firm, one afternoon and he mentioned that I was moving back to New York. She'd mentioned that they were looking to hire an associate and to submit my resume to her. Once I did, I received a call a week later to come in for an interview.

"You look pretty, Mom." Ruby grinned as she ate the pancakes my mother made for her.

"Thank you, sweetheart." I kissed her head.

"You look nervous." My mom handed me a cup of coffee.

"I am. This is Wolfe & Associates we're talking about. I have to nail this interview."

"You'll do great. You always do." A smile crossed her lips.

I took a few more sips from my cup and set it on the counter.

"Have fun with Grandma, Ruby. I'll be back in a while."

"Bye, Mom. Good luck!" She held her crossed fingers up to me.

I blew her a kiss. "Thanks, sweetheart."

***

I entered through the doors of the building on East 82nd Street and took the elevator up to the 37th floor. When the doors opened, I stepped onto the black & white mosaic marble floor and a young blonde woman sitting behind a mahogany desk greeted me.

"Welcome to Wolfe & Associates. How may I help you?"

"I'm here for an interview."

"Your name?" A smile perched on her plump red lips.

"Allison Price."

Her perfectly manicured fingers viciously typed away on the keyboard as she stared at the monitor.

"Ah yes. Here you are. You may have a seat right over there and I'll let Marie know you're here."

"Thank you."

I took a seat on the elongated couch as my belly twisted in a knot.

"Allison?" A young woman with a warm smile asked.

"Yes." I stood up.

"Hi. I'm Marie, Mr. Wolfe's secretary. It's nice to meet you." She extended her hand.

"Thank you. It's nice to meet you as well." I placed my hand in hers.

"Follow me and I'll take you to the conference room."

I followed her down the long hallway and into conference room one.

"Go ahead and have a seat. Elijah and Ms. Wolfe will be in shortly. May I get you some coffee or water?"

"No, thank you. I'm fine."

I inhaled a deep breath as I sat down in one of the high back gray leather chairs. A moment later, a tall and handsome man entered the room.

"Allison, it's nice to meet you. I'm Elijah Wolfe." He held out his hand.

Standing up, I placed my hand in his.

"It's nice to meet you, Mr. Wolfe." I smiled.

"My mother will be joining us in a few minutes," he spoke as he sat down in the seat across from me and opened up the file folder he had in his hand. "You previously worked for Roth & Associates in Chicago?"

"Yes."

"May I ask why you left?"

"I needed to move back to New York." I folded my hands on the table.

"Sorry I'm late. You must be Allison. I'm Caitlin Wolfe. It's so nice to meet you." A smile crossed her face as she extended her hand to me.

"Likewise, Ms. Wolfe."

"Your father has told me a lot about you. I want to say how sorry I am for your loss."

"Thank you. I appreciate it." I could feel the sting of tears rising.

"Loss?" Elijah looked at me.

"The reason I moved back to New York, Mr. Wolfe, was because my husband passed away a year ago. I grew up here and my family is here."

"I'm sorry for your loss, Miss Price."

"I gave your boss, Harry, a call the other day and he had nothing but stellar things to say about you. He was quite upset that you quit. He also told me that he offered you a substantial pay raise to stay and you turned it down," Caitlin spoke.

"That's because I needed to move back here. Not just for me, but for my daughter."

"You have a daughter?" Elijah asked.

"Yes. She's nine years old."

"I have a six-month-old daughter at home, and as a parent, I would also put her best interests first."

I gave him a small smile. "Both sets of her grandparents are here as well as her uncle. She needs to be surrounded by her family."

"I agree." He softly smiled.

"And family is very important. I don't know what I'd do without my boys. I think you're a perfect fit for our firm," Caitlin said. "If you accept the position, you'll be working under Elijah. He'll show you how we do things around here." She smirked. "Also, if you accept the position, we'll need you to start right away. Say, tomorrow at nine a.m. Would that be a problem?"

"No. Not at all." I grinned.

"Excellent." Elijah smiled.

"Perfect." Caitlin stood up and extended her hand. "Welcome to Wolfe & Associates."

"Thank you. Thank you so much." I lightly shook her hand.

"Elijah will go over everything with you, introduce you to the staff, and show you your office. In the meantime, I have a meeting with a client."

CHAPTER 7

Nathan

I opened my eyes to the sound of a text message coming through on my phone. Grabbing it off the nightstand, I saw I had a text from Mason.

"Bro, I'll swing by your place around one and we can go get our tuxedos."

Looking at the time, it was ten a.m.

"I'm just getting up and heading for a run. Care to join me?"

"Can't bro. Amelia is still here and we're having breakfast. Another time."

"I take it your date went well then."

"I'll tell you about it later."

Climbing out of bed, I pulled on a pair of sweatpants and a tank. Walking into the bathroom, I splashed some cold water on my face, fixed my hair and then brushed my teeth. After putting on my sneakers, I glanced at the island where the paper sat that I wrote on last night. Grabbing it, I folded it and placed it in my pocket. Stepping inside the elevator, I pushed the button to the lobby. It stopped on the twenty-second floor. When the doors opened, that same little girl stood there and narrowed her eye at me.

"You again," she spoke as she stepped inside.

"My feelings exactly, kid. Why do we keep running into each other? And why is it you're always by yourself?"

"I'm going down to the art room. My grandma is on the phone and said she'll be down in a minute. She's going to paint a picture with me."

"Where's your mom?"

"She's at a job interview."

"Ah. Hopefully she gets the job. Today's your lucky day."

"Why is that?" She looked up at me.

Reaching in my pocket, I pulled out the folded piece of paper.

"Here's the list of everyone that lives in the building."

With a narrowed eye, she took it from me, unfolded it, read it, and then handed it back to me.

"I can't believe you actually did that," she laughed as the doors opened to the lobby and we both stepped out.

"I did it to prove to you that I'm not a liar."

"Why do you have to prove anything to a nine-year-old?" She continued laughing as she walked towards the art room.

"Listen here, you little brat. It's obvious your mother hasn't taught you any manners. Your lack of respect is appalling." I followed behind her.

"I don't like you, Nathan. So do me a favor and don't talk to me again." She stuck her tongue out at me and then ran into the art room.

I was straight up fuming as I left the building and started my run. How dare she? What a brat. I could only imagine what kind of mother she had. And when I meet her, I'm going to tell her what a disrespectful child she was raising.

I ran the mile to Central Park and kept running as I listened to my favorite band: The Beatles. As I was running, this super-hot chick in skintight booty shorts and a sports bra gave me a flirty smile as she ran past me. I turned around and ran backwards for a moment as I stared at her fine ass. Damn. I needed to get home and take a cold shower.

After we got fitted and ordered our tuxedos, Mason and I headed to Tavola in Hell's Kitchen for some pizza.

"Fill me in on your date last night," I said as I brought the beer bottle up to my lips.

"It was nice. She was nice. The sex was nice."

"Are you going to be 'nice' about it when you tell her you don't want to see her again?" I smirked.

"I already kind of told her that my work schedule is crazy for the next month."

"What did she say?"

"She said she'd love to see me again and to call her when I have some free time."

"And now you'll ghost her." I let out a chuckle.

"Pretty much." He grinned as he drank his beer. I really have no interest in seeing her again. How was your run this morning?"

"Aside from running into that smart mouth little brat, it was fine."

"Who?" His brows furrowed. "You mean that little girl in your building?"

"Yes. Let me tell you what happened. I made a list of all the tenants in the building and put it in my pocket for when I saw her again. I was on my way down for a run when the elevator stopped on her floor. She stepped inside and I handed her the list. She proceeded to laugh and basically mocked me for doing it and then asked why I felt the need to prove myself to a nine-year-old."

Mason let out a laugh as he practically choked on his beer.

"Damn, Nathan."

"It gets better. I told her it was obvious that her mother didn't teach her any manners and that her lack of respect was appalling. You know what she did?"

"I can only imagine."

"She told me she didn't like me and to never talk to her again, and then the little brat stuck her tongue out at me."

"Holy shit." He continued to laugh.

"It's not funny." I pointed my finger at him. "In fact, I'm going to find out which apartment she lives in and then I'm having a little chat with her mother."

"Bro, come on. She's nine. Let it go. What is going on with you? You've been acting weird ever since that trip to Chicago. Does this have something to do with that girl you met in the airport rejecting you?"

"No." My brows furrowed.

"I think it does. First her and now this nine-year-old who can't stand you. You've had more rejection in the last week than your whole life." He laughed.

"You're an asshole, little brother. If we weren't in a public place, I'd fucking throw you to the ground."

"Yeah. Yeah. Anyway, we need to finalize our plans for Elijah's bachelor party."

"I've been thinking about that." I smirked.

After we left Tavola, I hailed a cab home. Mason was right. I did need to let it go as far as that little brat was concerned, but something inside me was hell bent on having that chat with her mother. Maybe I just wanted to see for myself what kind of person was raising that kid.

"Good day, Nathan." Vincent tipped his hat as he held the door open for me.

"Hey, Vincent. You know that little girl and her mom who just moved in not too long ago?"

"Yes."

"Whose apartment did they take over? I wasn't aware one had become available."

"Mrs. Fritz. She had to be transferred to an assisted living home. It happened when you were gone that week to Paris."

"Ah. That explains why I haven't seen her around. Thanks, Vincent." I patted his shoulder.

I stepped into the elevator and took it up to the twenty-second floor. After I knocked on the door of apartment 2210, I placed my hands in my pockets. Within a few moments, the door opened, and that little brat stood there, staring at me with wide green eyes.

"Is your mother home?" I asked.

Before she could respond, I heard a woman's voice.

"Ruby who is at—" Suddenly, she stopped when she saw me. She stood there in shock as did I.

"Allison?"

"Nathan? What the hell? Ruby, go to your room for a bit."

The child turned around and ran as fast as she could.

"What are you doing here? How the hell do you know where I live? Oh my God. You tracked me down!"

"Hold on a second." I put my hand up. "I didn't track you down. I live in this building. Up on the twenty-fifth floor to be exact."

CHAPTER 8

Allison

"You live here?" I asked. "In this building?"

"Yes. I'm in apartment 2508. I had a couple run ins with your kid and I wanted to have a little chat with her mother. I didn't know it would be you. But now it all makes sense." He shook his head.

"What makes sense?" She narrowed her eye at me.

"Nothing. I'm sorry to have bothered you." He turned and headed towards the elevator.

"Wait a second!" I voiced loudly as I ran after him. "What do you mean you had a couple of run ins with Ruby?"

The doors to the elevator opened, he stepped inside and then turned and looked at me.

"All I'm going to say is the apple doesn't fall far from the tree."

Before I could say a word, the doors closed. Pushing the button, I tried to stop it from going up so I could get an explanation from him. What the hell was he talking about? I went back inside my apartment and gripped the edge of the marble island. I couldn't believe he lived in the same building. Out of all the damn apartment buildings in New York City, I had to move into the one where he was at.

"Ruby!" I shouted. "Come out here, please."

"Is he gone?" she asked as she looked around.

"Yes. Now I want you to tell me what's going on? He said he had a couple of run ins with you. Explain yourself right now, young lady."

She lowered her head and began to tell me.

"Ruby." I walked over to her, bent down and lightly grasped her shoulders. "You know that wasn't nice."

"I know, Mom. I'm sorry."

"Well, you need to right this wrong and you know what you have to do, right?"

"Yes." She nodded her head.

"Go get your shoes on."

We took the elevator up to the twenty-fifth floor and stood outside the door of apartment 2508. After knocking, I grabbed hold of Ruby's hand. The door opened and Nathan stood there glaring at both of us without saying a word.

"Ruby has something she would like to say to you."

"Come on in." He gestured.

"I'm sorry for what I said, and I'm sorry for sticking my tongue out at you. It won't happen again."

He knelt down so he was at her level and extended his hand to her.

"I accept your apology, Ruby." He smiled and my heart started to flutter.

"Thank you, Nathan." She placed her hand in his.

"Ruby, go down to the apartment. I'll be there in a few minutes."

She opened the door and walked out.

"The more I thought about, I know exactly what you meant when you said the apple doesn't fall far from the tree. It must be the effect you have on women," I spoke with irritation.

"That's where you're wrong, love. I have the opposite effect on women. Most of the time I can't get away from them fast enough. So maybe it's you who has the problem." A smirk crossed his lips.

"You know what, Nathan, I thought I saw the last of you at the airport. But since we're living in the same building, it's inevitable that we'll run into each other. Let's make an agreement that neither one of us will acknowledge the other.

"Fine with me," he spoke.

"Good." I turned around and opened the door.

He lightly grabbed hold of my arm and spun me around. His face was mere inches from mine as his sexy green eyes stared into me. My breath hitched and my heart started racing.

"We'll just pretend we never met," he spoke in a low voice.

"Good idea."

He let go of my arm, and I walked out of his apartment, shutting the door behind me and trying to catch my breath as I stepped into the elevator. When I went back to my place, I found Ruby sitting on the couch playing her Nintendo Switch.

"Are you okay, Mom?"

"Of course, sweetheart. Why wouldn't I be?" I asked as I picked up the blanket from the floor and began folding it.

"Just making sure."

I put the blanket away and kissed the top of her head.

"I'm going to take a shower," I spoke.

I walked into the bathroom and shut the door. After turning on the shower, I closed the lid to the toilet, sat down, placed my hands in my face and began to cry.

CHAPTER 9

ONE WEEK LATER

*N*athan

I hadn't seen Allison or Ruby all week, which was fine with me. I still couldn't wrap my head around the fact that she lived in the same building. She looked just as beautiful that day I saw her at her apartment as she did at the airport. I didn't tell my brothers about our recent encounter because I didn't want to hear their shit.

I was just getting ready to head out the door when I heard a knock. Opening it, a guy in a pair of blue dress pants and a polo shirt stood there.

"Can I help you?"

"Are you Nathan Wolfe?"

"Yes."

He handed me an envelope.

"You've been served," he spoke and then walked away.

"Hey! I ran after him. "What the hell is this?"

"Open it and find out."

He stepped into the elevator, the doors shut, and he was gone. Shaking my head, I opened the envelope as I stepped back into my apartment.

"You've got to be fucking kidding me."

Pulling my phone from my pocket, I immediately called Elijah.

"What's up, Nathan?"

"Elijah, I need your help. I'm being sued."

"What?! What for?"

"Sexual harassment."

"Shit, Nathan. Get to my office now."

"I'm on my way. Hey, don't mention this to Mom."

"Just get here as fast as you can." He sighed.

I stepped into the building and took the elevator up to Elijah's office. The moment the doors opened, I saw my mother standing there.

Shit.

"Nathan, darling." She grinned. "What are you doing here?"

"Hey, Mom." I kissed her cheek. "I was in the area and thought I'd drop by to see you and Elijah."

"Aw, you're so sweet. I'm on my way out but Elijah is in his office."

"Thanks, Mom. I'll talk to you later."

Phew. Dodged that bullet.

Letting out a deep breath, I walked down the hallway and found Marie sitting at her desk.

"Hey, Marie."

"Hey, Nathan. Elijah said you were on your way over and to wait for him in his office. He's with a client in the conference room."

"Thanks." I gave her a small smile.

After stepping inside, I took a seat behind his desk and picked up the picture of him, Aspen and Mila. As I was setting it down, the door opened, and my jaw dropped.

"Nathan?" Allison asked in shock as she stood there and stared at me.

"What are you doing here?" My eye narrowed at her.

"I work here."

"Wait a minute. You work here? You work for my mother and brother?"

"Your mother and brother? Your last name is Wolfe?"

"Yes. What are you? A secretary? Paralegal?"

"I'm a lawyer."

I sighed as I leaned back in Elijah's chair and slowly shook my head.

"Well if you're looking for Elijah, he's with a client," I said.

"I know. He asked me to come down and meet with his brother until he was finished. I had no idea *you* were his brother."

"Oh hell no. I'm not discussing this with you. Where's Aspen?"

"She's at home. They're leaving for their trip today."

"Shit. I forgot they were leaving. Sorry, sweetheart, but this is a personal matter."

"Hand over the summons, Nathan. I already know you're being sued for sexual harassment." She held out her hand with a smirk across her face.

"Goddamn it. Elijah just couldn't keep his mouth shut."

"Would you have preferred he told your mother instead? Hand it over and let me take a look."

I sighed as I reluctantly handed over the summons. Needless to say, I was more than humiliated.

"Good. The two of you already met," Elijah spoke as he walked into the office."

"You and I are going to have a nice little chat, alone." I narrowed my eye at him.

Allison handed the summons over to Elijah and he took a look at it.

"Who is this Alessandra Rivera?" He glanced at me. "She's suing you for five hundred thousand dollars."

"She's a flight attendant, and yes, I know how much she's suing me for. This is bullshit."

"Why is she claiming sexual harassment?"

"How the hell do I know? The most I'd ever done was talk to her. In fact, I'd only flown with her a handful of times."

"Were you suggestive in your conversations?" Elijah asked.

"Fuck no. You know damn well I don't mess around with flight attendants for this very reason." I pointed at him.

"He doesn't," Allison chimed in. "In fact, there is a witness, another flight attendant, who can vouch for him."

I stared at her in disbelief that she actually believed me.

"How do you know that?" Elijah's brows furrowed.

"She told me on the flight to Chicago. This is isn't the first time your brother and I have met. The first time was at the airport, which he neglected to inform me during lunch that he was also the pilot for my flight."

"Wait a second." He laughed and glanced over at me. "Allison is the psycho chick you told us about?"

Shit.

"Psycho chick? Really, Nathan!"

"Thanks a lot, dickwad!"

"Okay. Both of you calm down. Nathan, don't worry about this. It won't even make it to court. Allison, call this woman's attorney and set up depositions for next week when I get back. Dig up every last bit of information you can on her. Meanwhile, tell me about this flight attendant that told you Nathan doesn't screw around with the flight attendants."

"When I heard him introduce himself over the speaker before the plane took off, I was shocked because I recognized his voice. So I gave his description to the attendant and she confirmed it was him." She narrowed her eyes at me. "Then she said he can be mysterious when he wants to be, and it was too bad he didn't mess around with flight attendants. She proceeded to tell me that she considered changing careers just to hook up with him."

I couldn't help but smile when I heard that. Not that I was surprised.

"Do you remember the name of this flight attendant?" Elijah asked her.

"I didn't catch her name. She was about five foot five, short blonde hair, blue eyes."

"That's Elizabeth Dushay." I grinned.

Elijah rolled his eyes.

"Write her name down as a character witness," he said to Allison.

"Allison's going to be working on your case with me and gathering all the information we're going to need while I'm in Florida. Like I said, bro," he hooked his arm around me, "this will all go away soon."

"It better. That woman is lying."

"Are you one hundred percent sure you don't know why she would do this?" my brother asked.

"Now that I'm thinking about it, there was one night during a layover where she was coming on to me. If she wasn't a flight attendant, I would have taken her up on her offer. But you know where I stand, Elijah."

"I know, little brother. Don't worry. We'll get it straightened out. Thank you, Allison. You can start gathering the information we're going to need to get this case thrown out."

"Of course," she spoke to Elijah and then looked at me before walking out of the office.

"I don't want her working on this. Do you remotely have a clue how humiliating this is for me?"

"Water under the bridge, Nathan."

"No, Elijah, it's not water under the bridge. She and her daughter live in my building. And we had a few words last week about how disrespectful her kid is. She can't stand me."

"She believed you didn't sexually harass that flight attendant, didn't she?"

"She would have believed it if Elizabeth didn't say what she did."

"Listen, she's new to the firm and this is a great way for me to find out how skilled of a lawyer she really is."

"So you're just going to leave my fate in the hands of someone new so you can see if she's any good. Really, Elijah? Cause if that's the case, then I'll gladly let Mom handle it."

"It's not my fault you made a play for her at the airport and pissed her off. Maybe you should have told her you were the pilot." He smirked. "Don't worry, you know I have your back. I'm not going to let this case get any further. Anyway, I'm glad the two of you don't get along because now that she works for me, she's off limits. Understand?"

"Yeah. Loud and clear. You don't have to worry about that."

"Good." He patted my shoulder. "I have to get home. Our flight leaves in three hours and Aspen is already blowing up my phone."

"Shouldn't you be staying around since you're getting married in a month?"

"We want to spend some alone time with Mila before we leave for our honeymoon. Aspen is already freaking out about it."

CHAPTER 10

*A*llison

I went back to my office, took a seat and placed my hands on my head as I took in a deep breath. That man was a Wolfe and I was still in shock over it. We'd made an agreement not to acknowledge each other again, but now that Elijah had me working on his brother's case, that agreement became null and void. Even after everything that had transpired between us since the first day we'd met, I believed him on this, and I would do everything I could to prove his innocence.

As I was sitting at my desk, my phone rang with an unfamiliar number.

"Allison Price."

"Allison, It's Nathan Wolfe. Elijah gave me your number. I just got a call and my boss wants me to come in for a meeting about this lawsuit. What should I do?"

"When does he want you to come in?"

"First thing tomorrow morning."

"Okay. We'll go together. I should be there."

"Fine. I can pick you up at your apartment at nine. If that's okay."

"Nine is good. I'll let my secretary know that I'll be out of the office most of the morning."

"Okay. See you then." He ended the call.

I sighed as I set my phone down.

"Bailey, can you come in for a moment?"

"What's up?" She walked in with a smile.

"I'm going to be out of the office most of the morning tomorrow. I need to attend a meeting with Nathan Wolfe."

"Lucky." Her grin widened. "He's so hot. Don't you think? And such a flirt."

"Aren't you married?" I cocked my head at her.

"Yeah. But I can still look, and Nathan Wolfe is one fine man to gaze at. In fact, all the Wolfe brothers are. Have you met the youngest one yet? He's dreamy too."

"Okay. Okay." I laughed. "I haven't met the youngest one yet but I'm sure I will. Go back to your desk and try to cool off."

There was another Wolfe brother? Good lord.

I picked up my phone, brought up Nathan's phone number and stored it in my contacts as "Sexy Wolfe." Why I did that; I hadn't a clue. It was the first thing that came to mind. If I was going to be working on this case, I needed to bury everything that transpired between us and put my hostilities aside. Sighing, I dialed his number.

"Hello."

"Nathan, it's Allison. I know this is extremely short notice, but are you going to be home tonight?"

"I wasn't planning on it. Why?"

"I was hoping I could drop by and go over a few things with you about the lawsuit."

"What time were you thinking?"

"My brother and his wife are picking Ruby up for the night at six thirty so I can come up around seven."

"I'll make sure I'm home then."

"Are you sure? I don't want to disrupt your plans."

"My plans can be put on hold. I was just going to go out and get drunk to try and forget this mess. But I suppose I can do that at home."

"Oh. Okay. I'll see you later then."

I set down my phone and placed my face in my hands.

"Are you okay?" Bailey asked as she walked into my office.

"Yeah." I sighed. "Just tired."

"Uncle Rick," Ruby squealed when she opened the door.

"Come here, pretty girl." He smiled as he hugged her.

"Hi." I smiled as I walked up to him.

"Hi." He kissed my cheek.

"Where's Darla?"

"She got tied up in a meeting so she's going to meet us at the restaurant."

"Thanks for keeping Ruby tonight. She's really excited to spend some time with you and Darla."

"We're excited to spend time with her." He grinned as he tapped her nose.

I told Ruby to go get her overnight bag while I went into the kitchen to clean up.

"How are you, sis?"

"I'm okay."

"You sure about that?"

"I miss him, Rick." I could feel the tears in my eyes.

"I know you do." He wrapped his arms around me. "You'll always miss him, but you have to move on at some point."

"I am. I moved back here and got a new job."

"That's a start, but you know what I'm talking about."

"No." I broke our embrace. "Jared was the love of my life."

"I'm ready, Uncle Rick." Ruby came running into the kitchen with her bag.

"Then let's hit the road, little one. I'm starving."

"Me too!" She grinned. "Bye, Mom."

"Bye, sweetheart." I gave her a hug. "Be good for Uncle Rick and Aunt Darla."

"I will."

Suddenly she became quiet and I saw a sadness in her eyes.

"What's wrong?"

"Are you going to be okay here by yourself?" she asked with a pout.

Anguish rose up inside me knowing that she worried about me.

"Of course I will be." A smile crossed my lips. "Now go with Uncle Rick and have fun." I gave her another hug. "I love you."

"I love you, too, Mom."

As soon as they left, I went into the bedroom to change out of my work clothes. After slipping into a casual maxi dress because it was so freaking hot out, I ran a brush through my hair and freshened up my makeup.

CHAPTER 11

*N*athan

After Allison called, I ran to the store to pick up some things to make dinner for us. It was the least I could do since my awesome attorney of a brother ditched me and left my case in her hands until he got back from his trip. I'd admit I was surprised by her phone call asking to come over to my place. Maybe she was using the case as an excuse and she came to her senses about me. One could only hope. She was sexy as all fuck, and I would say and do anything to get her into my bed. Perhaps tonight that could be arranged. Especially with Ruby out of the picture. Elijah told me she was off limits. But one night in secret wouldn't hurt anyone.

As I walked into my building, carrying a couple bags of groceries, I heard Mason from behind.

"Hey, douchebag. I hope there's a bag of salt and vinegar chips in there."

Turning around, I smiled as he placed his hand on my shoulder.

"What are you doing here?"

"Returning your sweatshirt I borrowed a couple of months ago. Here, let me take one of those."

He grabbed one of the bags from my hand as we headed toward the elevator.

"Thanks."

"I thought you have your groceries delivered," he spoke as we stepped into the elevator.

"I do. But today I thought I'd go myself."

"Why?"

"I'm having a guest for dinner." I smirked.

"Is she hot, sexy and willing to please?" A grin crossed his lips.

"She's hot and sexy. As for willing to please, I highly doubt it. But I'm hoping after tonight, she'll change her mind."

I grabbed the key from my pocket and unlocked the door to my apartment.

"Who is this mystery woman you're cooking for?"

"Remember the woman from the airport I told you about?"

"Bro, you need to be more specific. You're always telling me about women from the airport."

"The one who cussed me out."

"Oh yeah. The psycho chick. No way. How did you manage to find her? And why?" His brow arched.

"Long story short. Remember the smart mouth kid in the elevator?"

"Yeah."

"She's her daughter and they both live in the building. But the real shocker is she's Elijah's new associate at the firm."

"Shut the fuck up. She works for Elijah and Mom?"

"Yep."

"If that's the case, then she's off limits. Didn't Elijah warn you already?"

I sighed as I unpacked the bags and began putting everything away.

"Yeah. He warned me. There's more to the story." I opened the fridge, pulled out a bottle of beer, opened it and handed it to him. "I'm being sued for sexual harassment."

"What?" He laughed. "By who?"

"Some bitch flight attendant that I turned down. I went to see Elijah about it today and of course he was rushing out of there because he and Aspen were leaving for Florida. He's having Allison gather as much info as she can while he's gone. Meanwhile, my boss called and wants me in his office tomorrow morning for a meeting. I told Allison and she's going with me. But she wants to talk to me about the case before tomorrow. So, she's coming up around seven."

"Why the fuck didn't you tell me any of this?"

"It just happened today. I haven't had a chance to."

"Well, don't worry about it. Elijah will take care of it. What did Mom say?"

"Mom doesn't know, and I don't want her to." I pointed my finger at him. "So don't say a word."

"She's Mom. She's going to find out."

"If and when she does, I'm hoping it'll be over with."

"She's going to be pissed, bro." He laughed.

"The only thing I'm focusing on tonight is Allison."

"But she has a kid."

"So." I shrugged. "It's not like I want a relationship with her. I only want to fuck her." A smile crossed my mouth.

"And if that happens and Elijah finds out?"

"Elijah isn't going to find out anything. She certainly won't tell him."

"Don't you think you're being a little premature? From what you told me, she can't stand you."

"She just doesn't know me yet." I winked.

"Good luck." He finished his beer.

Looking at the clock, I saw it was six fifty-five.

"You better get going. She'll be here in about five minutes."

Just as I said that, there was a knock at the door.

"Shit. She's early." I looked at Mason.

"Five minutes. Big deal. She probably can't wait to get in your pants."

"Get the fuck out of here."

I walked over to the door and opened it.

"Hey, Allison. Come on in."

"Nathan." She nodded.

"This is my baby brother, Mason."

"Hi, Mason. I'm psycho chick from the airport. I'm sure your brother has told you all about me." She extended her hand.

He couldn't contain his laughter and I was going to kill him.

"Nice to meet you, psycho chick." He placed his hand in hers. "I'll let you two get on with your meeting. I'll talk to you later, bro."

He walked out and I shut the door.

"Please, make yourself comfortable. I was just about to throw a couple of steaks on the grill."

"I'm not staying. I just came over to ask you a few questions." The tone in her voice was serious and I needed to lighten her mood.

"Well, I bought a steak for you and I'll answer your questions over dinner. Until then, I'm not saying a word." I gave her a smirk. "How do you like your steak? Wait. You do like steak, right? You're not a vegetarian, are you? Please for the love of god tell me you eat meat."

She let out a light laugh.

"I like my steak medium rare." Her lips formed a smile.

A laugh and a smile. So far, we were off to a good start and I was starting to feel confident about tonight.

"Two medium rare steaks coming right up." I winked as I took the steaks out on the terrace and put them on the grill.

"Is there anything I can help with?" she politely asked.

"Do you like sweet potatoes?"

"I do."

"Would you mind throwing them in the microwave? It'll be quicker than putting them in the oven."

"Sure. I can do that."

"Thanks. They're on the counter by the sink."

I stood at the grill, watching the steaks and her as she put the potatoes in the microwave. Every time I saw her, she was more beautiful. And that body. Damn. My cock was starting to misbehave. I saw her open the refrigerator and shake her head.

"What's wrong?" I asked from the terrace.

"You don't have cinnamon butter?"

"No. Why?"

"How does one eat a sweet potato without cinnamon butter?"

"To be honest, I never thought about it."

"Then you're in for a treat. I have some down in my apartment. I'll be right back."

"Okay. Just walk in when you get back."

As far as I was concerned, the only treat I wanted was between her long lean legs. The microwave had just gone off and the steaks were done. Putting them on a plate, I set the steaks on the island and took out the potatoes from the microwave. Reaching into the cabinet, I grabbed two plates, setting a steak and potato on each of them.

The door opened, and Allison walked inside holding up the tub of cinnamon butter with a grin on her face.

"Just in time. Dinner is ready," I spoke. Walking over to the wine rack, I pulled a bottle of Cabernet from it. "I have the perfect wine to go with this steak. You in?" I arched my brow as I held up the bottle.

"I'm in." Another beautiful smile crossed her lips.

We took our seats at the table and I watched as she cut into her steak.

"Wow. This is perfect, Mr. Wolfe. I didn't know you were a grill master."

"That's not the only thing I'm a master at." I winked.

Unfortunately, she didn't find that amusing, but nonetheless, I knew deep down inside she was curious.

"Down to business. Ask me whatever questions you'd like."

CHAPTER 12

A llison

I barely knew this man and now I was sharing a meal with him, again. I wasn't sure how Elijah would feel about this. But it was strictly business and it was my job to gather as much information as I could to help his brother.

"First, you have to put some of that cinnamon butter on your potato," I said.

"Ah yes. You did say I was in for a treat."

He grabbed his knife and placed it in the tub of butter. After spreading it on the potato, he took his fork and tasted it. I watched the reaction on his face and suddenly, I felt all kinds of fluttering in my belly.

"Damn. This is amazing. How have I never thought about this? Thank you."

"You're welcome. Now, down to business. I need you to tell me exactly what happened with this flight attendant named Alessandra?"

"Not much really. She was on a few of my flights and she flirted a lot."

"Did you flirt back?"

"No. I keep it very professional with the flight attendants."

"So you never once led any attendant to believe that you were interested in them?"

"Unfortunately, no. We were on a layover in Italy a few months back."

"How long was the layover?"

"Thirty-six hours. The crew was at the hotel and we were in the bar having a few drinks. Everyone was tired so they went up to their rooms. I wasn't tired and I wanted to see some sights before I had to fly back. Alessandra asked if she could come with me and I said yes. After a while, she started making advances towards me and said we should go back to my room to have some fun. I told her no and that I don't get involved with the flight staff. She said she understood, and I thought everything was cool. We went back to the hotel, and I went to my room and she went to hers. About thirty minutes later, there was a knock on my door. When I opened it, she stood there in one of the hotel robes holding a bottle of wine. She pushed past me and stepped inside the room. I told her that this was inappropriate, and she had to leave. She set the bottle of wine down and she threw herself at me and smashed her mouth against mine. Immediately, I pulled away, grabbed hold of her arm and tossed her out of my room. She looked at me with this crazy look in her eye and said, 'Nobody rejects me.' Then she went back to her room. When I returned to New York, I told management that I didn't want her on my schedule again."

"Did they ask why?"

"I told them that she'd be a better fit on other flights. They didn't really question it."

"Okay. Here's how I see it. She's going to pretty much tell the same story, but spin it around to make it look like you were the one coming on to her and she said no. And once she rejected your advances, you made sure she didn't fly with you again. Hence the reason for the sexual harassment charge. Don't be surprised tomorrow if the airline suspends you until this is over."

"What? They can't do that. I didn't do anything wrong."

"It's a case of he said she said."

"And you think they'll side with her?"

"Maybe. I'm not really sure. We'll have to wait and see. On another note, you can cook a mean steak. This is really good."

"Thanks. I need something stronger than wine. You?" he asked as he got up and walked over to the mini bar that sat in the corner of the living room.

"I'm good. Listen, Nathan, try not to stress over this. It's all going to be okay. Elijah is a brilliant lawyer and he's not going to let Alessandra win."

"And what about you? Are you a brilliant lawyer? You're the one handling this right now while my brother is off playing house," he spoke with irritation.

"I've been told I'm a good lawyer."

"I don't need good! I need the best and the best is Elijah!" he shouted. "This woman is fucking lying through her teeth!" He threw the liquid gold down the back of this throat.

"And I'll gather the evidence we need to prove it," I spoke as I grabbed our plates from the table.

"Leave that. I'll clean it up later."

"No. You cooked, and I'll clean up. That's how—" I stopped mid-sentence.

"That's how what?"

"Nothing," I quietly spoke as I rinsed off the plates and put them in the dishwasher.

Suddenly, there was a knock at the door.

"Nathan, are you home?"

"Shit. It's my mother." He rolled his eyes.

Walking over to the door, he opened it and Caitlin stepped inside.

"Nathan Michael Wolfe, we need to talk."

The moment she saw me in the kitchen, she stopped.

"Hello, Caitlin," I spoke with nervousness.

"Allison, darling. What are you doing here? I didn't know you and my son knew each other."

"Oh. Umm—"

CHAPTER 13

Nathan
"She's here because of Elijah. She also lives in the building. What are you doing here?"

"Well," she sighed as she set her purse down, "I came across a tidbit of information today. I'm assuming Allison already knows since you said she's here because of Elijah. Nathan, what did you do?"

"I did nothing. That woman is lying. And how did you hear about it? Elijah?"

"No. I overheard a couple of the girls talking about it in the office, so I confronted them."

"Great." I rolled my eyes.

"Don't worry. I put a stop to it. And of course that woman is lying." She placed her hand on my cheek. "Allison, why did Elijah involve you in this?"

"He wants me to gather all the information I can before he gets back," she spoke.

"Okay. Whatever cases you're currently working on, I want you to stop. This case takes top priority. Understand me?"

"Yes, Caitlin."

"Good. Don't worry, darling, this will all go away." She hugged him. "But regardless, I'm angry with you for not coming directly to me with this. Would you care to explain yourself?" Her brow raised.

I stood there looking away with my hands tucked into my pants pockets.

"Well, Nathan?"

"You're my mother." I gestured to her. "How could I tell you that some lunatic woman was suing me for sexual harassment? It's embarrassing."

"You're right, darling, I am your mother. I gave birth to you. Thirty-six hours of painstaking labor and the fact that you ripped me in two during your journey into this world."

"Really, Mom?" I cocked my head.

"My point is I will always have your back and I will love you no matter what you've done. You know that. So, I'll admit I'm hurt that you chose to shut me out of this situation you're in."

I wrapped my arms around her. "I'm sorry, Mom. You're right. I should have come to you."

"Just don't do it again. You know you can talk to me about anything." She broke our embrace and gave me a smile. "Now that we've settled that, I have a bed date with a hot district attorney because I have to fly out in the morning to Washington." She gave me a wink.

"Mother, please. Jesus." I put my hand up.

She kissed my cheek and grabbed her purse. "You two enjoy the rest of your evening. I'm trusting you, Allison. In Elijah's absence, you do whatever it is you need to. Legal or not." Her brow arched. As soon as she walked out the door, I let out a long sigh. Suddenly, my phone rang, and Elijah was Facetiming me. Without even thinking about Allison being here, I answered it.

"To what do I owe the pleasure, brother?" I cocked my head.

"I wanted to let you know that Mom knows about the lawsuit. Apparently, she heard it around the office."

"Yes. I know. She already paid me a little visit."

"Oh shit. Are you okay?" He laughed.

"As well as can be expected during this turbulent time in my life."

Allison walked over to the table, grabbed her glass of wine and finished it off.

"Allison?" Elijah spoke.

"Hey, Elijah." She smiled into the phone.

Shit.

"I'm going to get going. Thanks for dinner and I'll see you in the morning." She grabbed her purse and walked out the door.

Fuck.

"What the hell was Allison doing in your apartment?" Elijah's brow arched. "And what did she mean 'thanks for dinner?' I swear to God, Nathan."

"Dude, calm the fuck down. She asked if she could come up to ask me a few questions for the case. I threw a couple of steaks on the grill. No big deal."

"It is a big deal when you also served her wine!" he loudly voiced.

"Well, it's your fault." I pointed at him. "You put her on this case while you're off lollygagging in Florida! She's just doing her job."

"I'm trusting you to keep your hands to yourself."

"Don't worry about it. I'll be a good little boy, Daddy."

"Don't be a smartass and try to forget about this mess. I'll clear it up when I get back. I have to go. Stay cool, bro."

"Yeah. Trying to."

I ended the call and sighed. Thanks to Elijah he ruined my potential night of hot sex with Allison. *Cockblocker.*

Before I went down to Allison's apartment, I got up early, went for a run, lifted some heavy weights at the gym, showered and then went to pick her up. Knocking on the door, the sharp intake of my breath startled me when she opened it. My breath literally confined me in its grip.

"Good morning." The corners of her mouth slightly curved upward.

"Morning."

"Come on in for a second. I just have to grab my purse and briefcase."

She looked sexy as fuck in her off white tailored pant suit. Shit. Placing my hand in my pocket, I tried to calm my rising cock.

"Now remember, whatever the airline hands you because of this lawsuit, just accept it and let me do the talking," she spoke as we sat in the back of the cab.

"Easy for you to say. It's utter bullshit if they suspend me."

We reached the office of my boss, Dan Hartwig. I wouldn't lie and say I wasn't nervous, because I was.

"Nathan, good to see you." Dan flashed a smile as we stepped inside his office. "Who's this?"

Allison extended her hand. "Allison Price. Nathan's attorney."

"Nice to meet you." Dan placed his hand in hers. "I'm not sure why you're here though."

"I'm protecting the interest of my client."

"Where's your brother?" Dan asked in confusion.

"He's away at the moment. Miss Price is filling in for him until he gets back."

The three of us took a seat and Dan sighed as he cupped his hands on his desk.

"In light of this sexual harassment suit filed against you from one of the flight attendants, the airline has no choice but to suspend you without pay until the matter is cleared up. I'm sorry, Nathan."

A sick feeling rose from the pit of my stomach. As I began to speak, Allison interrupted.

"Mr. Hartwig, has Mr. Wolfe had any prior warnings about his behavior since he started working for your company?"

"No. Not a single one. In fact, he's an excellent pilot and employee. The airline has to take every sexual harassment suit very seriously regardless of the employee's history. To be honest, I don't believe what this woman says to be true, but in any case, she is our employee as well."

"She's a lying bitch!" I snapped and Allison placed her hand on my arm.

"Thank you, Mr. Hartwig. Is that all?"

"Yes. Nathan, I'm really sorry about this. My hands are tied."

"I understand, Dan, but it's bullshit," I scowled.

The meeting ended, and as we walked out of the building, I asked her if she wanted to grab some breakfast.

"I'm starving. How about we grab some breakfast."

"Have you forgotten that I have to go to work?"

"You are working. I'm your client and we need to discuss my case over breakfast."

CHAPTER 14

Allison

I was hungry and having breakfast with him wouldn't be so bad. Afterall, we did have dinner together last night and I found it —rather nice. What he told me about him and Alessandra, I believed him. I could see it in his eyes, and I was pretty good at spotting when people were lying to me.

"Fine. We can have a quick breakfast. A quick one. Got it?" I arched my brow at him. "I have to get back to the office."

"Yes, ma'am. Quick isn't my specialty though. I like to take my time in everything I do." A smirk crossed his lips.

I rolled my eyes as we walked down the street to a small family owned diner.

"Table for two, please," Nathan spoke as we stepped inside.

Just as we were seated, my phone rang and Bailey, my secretary was calling.

"Hey, Bailey."

"Sorry to call you, Allison, but Mr. Thorne returned your call from yesterday."

"What did he say?"

"He scheduled depositions for tomorrow morning at nine a.m. at his office."

"What?! No. We can't do that. Elijah isn't back yet."

"And I think he got wind of that and that's why he wants it done immediately."

"Thanks for letting me know," I sighed.

I ended the call and quickly dialed a friend of mine whom I've known for years.

"What is going on?" Nathan asked as he sat across from me.

I held up my finger.

"Hey, Marco."

"Well hello there, pretty lady. To what do I owe the pleasure?"

"I need your help. It's urgent."

"Of course, Allison. Anything. What's going on?"

We spoke for a few moments and I ended the call.

"For the last time, what the fuck is going on?" Nathan asked with irritation.

"Alessandra's attorney scheduled the deposition for tomorrow morning at nine a.m."

"What? Why already?"

"Bailey thinks he got wind that Elijah is out of town." I sighed.

"Oh my God." He placed his hands on his head. "Elijah has to come back today. Shit. I can't even call my mother. She left this morning for Washington."

I picked up my phone and dialed Elijah. It went straight to voicemail, so I tried Aspen. No answer.

"Neither one is answering," I said as I picked up my coffee cup and took a sip from it.

"Of course they aren't. That's it. My career is over, ruined and destroyed because of that lying bitch and her snake of an attorney."

I swallowed hard when he said that.

"You don't trust me, do you?" I asked.

"Honestly, Allison, no. I'm sorry. I really am. I need my brother or my sister-in-law. Even my mother. They're better equipped to handle this case than you are."

I sat there with my jaw literally dropped to the floor. Slowly shaking my head, I got up and grabbed my purse and my briefcase.

"Where are you going?"

"I'm taking my un-equipped ass to the office. I'll text you the address of where to meet for the depositions later."

"Allison," he sighed, "I'm sorry."

"Save it for someone who cares, Nathan." I shot him a look as I walked out of the diner.

When I reached my office, I pulled out my phone and tried calling Elijah again. Straight to voicemail. Throwing my phone across my desk, I placed my hands on my hips and paced back and forth.

"You okay?" Bailey asked.

"Nathan doesn't trust me. He said I wasn't as equipped to handle this as his family was."

"He didn't mean it. He's just stressed. Is Elijah on his way back?"

"I can't get a hold of Elijah or Aspen. Both phones go to voicemail."

"Listen, Allison. I don't know you very well, but from the short time I've spent here at the office with you, I can tell you're a great lawyer. You can do this on your own. You don't need the Wolfes."

"Thanks, Bailey. I know I can do it. It's just the pressure of trying to live up to their expectations that's causing this undeniable amount of doubt. Not to mention that Nathan thinks I'm highly incapable."

"Then prove him wrong. And forget about the Wolfe's expectations. Just be you and do what you do best." A small smile framed her face.

Later that afternoon, Bailey stepped into my office to alert me that Elizabeth Dushay was waiting in the conference room. Grabbing the notepad from my desk, I headed down to meet with her.

"Miss Dushay." I extended my hand. "It's nice to see you again."

She cocked her head and placed her hand in mine as she stared at me.

"I remember you. You were on one of my flights," she spoke. "Chicago, right?"

"Yes. Thank you for coming in."

I took the seat across from her at the large rectangular table.

"How well do you know Alessandra Rivera?" I asked.

"Not very well. I've only worked with her a few times."

"You told me on the flight to Chicago that Mr. Wolfe doesn't date flight attendants. Do you remember our conversation?"

"Yeah. I remember. All of the flight attendants who have worked with Nathan for years know he has a hands-off policy."

"What do you mean by that?"

"If you're a flight attendant, you don't stand a chance with him. He's made it very clear that he doesn't get involved with us."

"Did he ever tell you why?"

"He just said it's a policy of his and as much as we flight attendants hate it, we respect it. Like I told you on the flight to Chicago, I seriously considered switching careers just to go out with him. I mean, who wouldn't." She bit down on her bottom lip.

"How is his behavior on flights?" I asked.

"Strictly professional. I've tried flirting with him several times, but he just dismisses it. In fact, we all have."

"And what about layovers?"

"He pretty much goes off on his own. Half the time he doesn't even stay at the hotel."

"Where does he stay?"

"Rumor has it that he has a variety of women he stays with in different parts of the country/world."

"Seriously?"

"Yeah. Lucky women."

"Thank you, Miss Dushay. I think we're finished here." I stood up and extended my hand.

"You're welcome. If you need anything else, just let me know."

CHAPTER 15

Allison

I was sitting at my desk when my phone rang, and Marco was calling.

"Hey, Marco."

"Allison, I have some information for you on a Miss Alessandra Rivera."

"Excellent. Tell me it's something good."

We talked for several minutes while I took down some notes and then I ended the call. Just as I set my phone down, it rang again and this time it was Elijah.

"Finally," I spoke to myself. "Elijah."

"Allison, I'm sorry. We've been in the ER all day with Mila. She has an ear infection."

"Oh no. I'm sorry to hear that."

"We finally got her to go to sleep. What's going on? Aspen said you called her a couple times as well."

"Mr. Thorne, Miss Rivera's attorney, scheduled the deposition for tomorrow morning at nine a.m."

"What the fuck. What's the rush?"

"I think he got wind that you and your mother are out of town."

"That bastard. I'll call him."

"No, don't. Let him go ahead with his plan. I have some information and you can attend the meeting via Facetime."

"That'll have to do for now. There's no way we can get on a plane with the baby having an ear infection right now and I'm not leaving Aspen here alone to deal with her. Call me when it starts."

"I will. I need to go. I have another call I have to make regarding the case."

※

After leaving the office, I went over to my brother's house to have dinner with them and Ruby. He had called earlier in the day to ask if they could keep Ruby another night because they were having a lot of fun. I agreed since I had to be in depositions in the morning.

As I walked into my building, my belly twisted when I saw Nathan standing in front of the elevator. I hadn't spoken to him since I walked out of the diner this morning.

"Hey," I nervously spoke as I stood next to him clutching the strap to my purse.

"Hey." He glanced over at me with his hands tucked tightly into his pants pockets. "You talk to Elijah today?"

"I did. He'll be joining us via Facetime tomorrow."

"I know. He told me."

The doors opened and we both stepped inside.

"I know you're still mad at me for this morning, but do you think we could go together tomorrow?"

I stood there in silence for a moment.

"I guess that means no." He sighed.

The elevator stopped on my floor and when the doors opened, I stepped out and turned to face him.

"Pick me up at eight fifteen."

A light smile crossed his lips as he gave me a nod.

※

The next morning, I stared at myself in the mirror while taking in long deep breaths. I was ready and I pushed out any doubts or fears that resided in me. I could do this. It was nothing but another case. A case in which I would walk in and expose that lying bitch for the fraud she was. Nathan told me I was incapable of handling this and I was going to prove him wrong.

I was startled out of my deep thoughts by a knock on the door. Walking over to it, I opened the door and found Nathan standing there holding two coffee cups in his hand.

"Good morning. I figured you could probably use this." He handed me the cup.

"Thanks. I do."

I grabbed my purse and my briefcase, and we headed out the door.

"You look great," he spoke as we stepped into the elevator.

"Thank you." I could feel the heat rise in my cheeks.

I tried not to notice how sexy he looked in his tailored black suit, but it was impossible not to. Damn it.

"Mr. Thorne will go first and ask you a bunch of questions. Just answer them truthfully and calmly. Please for the love of god don't get all worked up."

"I won't. I'll be on my best behavior. But only because you asked me to." He smirked. "I spoke with Elijah again last night and he told me that he's flying back tomorrow, and he'll be taking over the case."

"I'm sure you were happy to hear that."

"Again, I'm sorry for what I said yesterday morning, but—"

"But you still don't trust me and think I'm incapable of handling your case. I know, Nathan. Believe me when I say I don't care what you think. I know my capabilities and I know how to practice the law. If you don't think I'm good enough, that's your problem, not mine."

"Okay then. Clearly you're still pissed off."

"How about I criticize your piloting abilities?" I arched my brow at him.

"Seriously? You have no idea about my abilities as a pilot."

"And you don't have any idea of my abilities as a lawyer. Just because my last name isn't Wolfe, doesn't mean I don't know how to do my job. We're here. Let's go and get this shit show over with."

We stepped inside the building located at 90 and Park Avenue and took the elevator up to the twenty-eighth floor.

"Good morning. We're here for Mr. Thorne," I spoke.

"Well, hello." The blonde receptionist behind the desk smiled as she stared at Nathan. "Your name?" she asked him.

"Hello there, beautiful. I'm Nathan Wolfe." He grinned back at her.

I sighed as I rolled my eyes.

"Please let Mr. Thorne know that Allison Price and Nathan Wolfe are here for depositions."

"One moment, please." She picked up the phone sitting on her desk. "Mr. Thorne is ready for you. Follow me."

She stepped out from behind her desk and led us to the conference room. I smacked Nathan's arm as I caught him staring at her ass in her little black tight skirt.

"Ouch."

"Could you please show some professionalism. Or is that too much to ask?"

"Someone took their nasty pills this morning. I just hope you direct that nastiness to the appropriate party." The corners of his mouth curved upward.

Rolling my eyes, we stepped into the conference room.

"You must be Miss Price," a large man with white hair asked as he extended his hand.

"Mr. Thorne. Nice to meet you."

"You two may have a seat." He gestured to the other side of the table.

"I'm not sitting across from her," Nathan whispered.

"Sit down." I spoke through gritted teeth. "Before we get started, I have a phone call to make."

"Miss Price, now is not the—"

"Good morning, Elijah," I spoke as I propped my iPad up.

"Good morning, Allison. Nathan. Harold, good to see you." Elijah smiled."

"Elijah." The tone in his voice wasn't a pleasant one.

CHAPTER 16

Allison

"Miss Rivera, who is Professor Jared Simmons?" I asked.

"What relevance does this have, Miss Price?" Harold asked.

"A lot of relevance. Miss Rivera?"

"I was his assistant at the University of Chicago a few years ago."

I silently smiled at the nervousness in her voice.

"You filed a sexual harassment suit against him. Correct?"

"Yes. He had me transferred out of his department after I refused to sleep with him. Just like Nathan did."

I placed my hand on Nathan's arm because I knew he was going to say something.

"I want that comment stricken from the record." I glanced over at the court reporter.

"So you're saying you never slept with Professor Simmons?"

"No. He's married, and I would never."

"Then how do you explain this?" I asked as I pulled out a photo of them hand in hand in the lobby of the Ritz Carlton.

She swallowed hard as she looked at the picture.

"I have sworn testimony from Professor Simmons himself stating that the two of you carried on an affair for over a year and it was when he refused to leave his wife that you filed the suit against him."

"What the hell does that have to do with this case, Miss Price?" Harold asked.

"A lot. Because when Miss Rivera doesn't get her way with a man, she screams sexual harassment."

"That is not true!" she yelled.

"I have a sworn statement by one of the other flight attendants that says Mr. Wolfe doesn't and has never engaged in sexual activity with any of the flight attendants. The flight crew knows he has a policy and a rule against that. I will subpoena every damn flight attendant Mr. Wolfe has ever worked with. This picture here tells us that Miss Rivera lied under oath in her previous lawsuit, and I'm prepared to go even further to show that she lied about that sexual harassment case and how she's lying about this one." I placed my hands on the table and leaned over, so I was staring her in the eyes. "Make no mistake, Miss Rivera, by the time this lawsuit is said and done, you will be buried so deep in the ground that you'll never climb your way out."

"Did you just threaten my client, Miss Price?" Harold shouted as he stood up from his chair.

"I wouldn't call it a threat, Harold." Elijah smiled. "Facts are facts. Now if you insist on taking this any further then be prepared for war. Nobody fucks with my family. Especially my brother."

He stared at Elijah for a moment and then looked at me.

"Will you excuse us for a moment?"

"Of course."

"Alessandra, come with me," he spoke.

As soon as they left the conference room, Nathan looked at me as he leaned back in his chair.

"Wow. You can be quite scary when you need to be." He grinned.

"Good job, Allison." Elijah spoke. "I couldn't have done it better myself."

"Thanks, Elijah."

A few moments later, Harold walked back into the conference room alone.

"Where's your client?" I asked. "I don't believe we're finished here."

"Miss Rivera has decided to drop the suit against Mr. Wolfe. She said she was drinking that night and may have been mistaken. Thank you for your time. My secretary will show you out," he spoke as he left the room.

"Excellent job, Allison. I have to go and see how Mila is doing. We'll talk when I get back. Since the suit has been dropped, there's no need for me to fly back tomorrow. Congratulations, Nathan."

"Thanks, bro. I'll see you soon."

I picked up my iPad and shoved it along with some files back into my briefcase.

"I can't believe it's over," Nathan spoke. "You were fantastic. I could kiss you right now."

"Please don't." I put my hand up. "A simple thank you is enough."

"Have dinner with me tonight," he spoke as we stepped into the elevator.

"I can't. I have plans."

"Then tomorrow night."

"Listen, Nathan," I said as the elevator opened to the lobby, "I'm not interested in having dinner with you. Not tonight, not tomorrow, not ever. I was your attorney on a case and that case is over. Now we go our separate ways. I'll draft a letter and send it to your employer telling them that she dropped the suit against you and your suspension is to be revoked immediately. Have a good day," I said as I climbed into a cab, shut the door and took in a deep breath.

CHAPTER 17

*N*athan

I stood there with my hands tucked into my pockets staring at the cab as it pulled away from the curb. What pissed me off the most was her attitude towards me. Maybe I was wrong to voice my opinion about her handling my case, but she needed to realize my reputation and career was on the line. Not to mention the fact that I felt abandoned by my family who were supposed to be there for me. Nonetheless, I hurt her feelings and I needed to make amends with her.

Pulling my phone from my pocket, I dialed my mother.

"Nathan, darling, is everything okay?"

"Hi, Mom. Allison got the lawsuit dropped. It's over."

"That's excellent news, Nathan. Obviously, I made the right decision in hiring her. I'll be home in a couple of days, and we'll celebrate the good news."

"Sounds good, Mom. I have to go. Have a safe flight home."

"Thank you, darling. Talk to you soon."

After ending the call, I decided to see if Mason was home.

"Hello," his sleepy voice answered.

"Get your lazy ass up. I'm on my way over with a couple of breakfast sandwiches from Sammy's."

"Don't you have depositions this morning?"

"It's done and over with. The lawsuit was dropped. I'll explain when I get there."

"Yeah. Okay, bro. I'll unlock the door, just walk in. I'm jumping in the shower."

On my way to Mason's, I stopped at Sammy's Diner and ordered two breakfast sandwiches and power smoothies to go. When I arrived at his apartment, I took out the sandwiches and set them on the table.

"Hey, bro. Congrats on the lawsuit being dropped." Mason fist bumped me. "Did Allison have something to do with it or did that chick decide to stop being a bitch?"

"Allison found some dirt on her and basically threatened to ruin her if she continued with the suit," I spoke as I pulled the chair out and took a seat.

"Wow. She sounds tough like Mom and Elijah."

"She is and I made a huge mistake. One I'm not sure she'll forgive me for."

"What did you do?"

I took a bite of my sandwich. "I basically told her that I didn't trust her to handle my case and I felt she was a little uncapable."

"Shit, Nathan. Why would you do that?"

"Because my reputation and career were on the line. I freaked out. Especially with Mom and Elijah out of town. I apologized but she didn't care. And when I asked her to dinner, she told me she wasn't interested. Not today, not tomorrow, not ever. Do you fucking believe that?"

"Yeah," he spoke as he sipped his smoothie. "You didn't believe in her without even knowing what kind of lawyer she was. The truth is, we're so used to Elijah and Mom being the big sharks that it's hard to know if anyone else would come close to being like them. I say give it up and move on."

"That's not an option for me. I need to make amends with her. Plus, I'm extremely attracted to her and I just can't let that go. I have a need, brother. And that need is to get her into my bed. Just one time is all I want. My curiosity is getting the best of me."

"Have you ever heard how curiosity killed the cat? Dude, once again do I need to remind you that she's off limits. Elijah will kick your ass if you sleep with one of his employees."

"What Elijah doesn't know won't hurt him. I have a plan."

"Jesus. What is it?"

"What's the one way to pull the heartstrings of a woman? What do women find sexier than anything else?"

"Enlighten me, please."

"A man who adores their kid."

"So you're going to use her kid to get to her?" His brow arched.

"If I have to, yes."

"That's low, Nathan. Even for you. What about the kid's father? Do you know anything about him?"

"No. I haven't gotten that far yet. She started to say something the other night at dinner and stopped. I'm guessing he's back in Chicago. Which also leads me to question why he would allow her to take Ruby and move out of state. He must be a total dick and a shit father."

"Maybe." He shrugged. "Just be careful, bro. I'd hate to lose you."

"Lose me how?" I furrowed my brows.

"When Elijah buries you six feet in the ground."

"Enough with Elijah." I leaned back in my chair as I finished off my smoothie. "Besides, Aspen will put him in his place if he gives me too hard of a time about it. But we're not going to mention any of this to Elijah, are we?" I cocked my head.

"Fuck no. I'm not getting involved in this one. You're on your own. But don't say I didn't warn you." He pointed his finger at me.

After I left Mason's apartment, I stopped by the florist on the way home and ordered a dozen white roses and had them sent to Allison's office with a card that read:

Allison,
Thank you again for today. I never should have doubted you and I'm truly sorry. Have dinner with me.

Sincerely yours,
Nathan

Later that evening, as I was about to walk out the door to meet some friends at the bar, my phone dinged with a text message from Allison.

"Thank you for the flowers. They're beautiful and look great sitting on my desk. P.S. Dinner is a no."

Shit.

"You're welcome, and I hope you'll think of me every time you look at them. P.S. Have dinner with me."

I knew she probably wasn't going to respond to my last text, so I shoved my phone in my pocket and headed out the door.

CHAPTER 18

ONE WEEK LATER

*N*athan

It felt good to be back up in the air again. Four days in a row and now I had the next eight days off. Four of which were vacation days. I walked into my apartment building in my pilot's uniform because I'd forgot to pack an extra pair of clothes to travel home in. When the doors opened, I saw Ruby standing there.

"Hey, Nathan." She smiled as she stepped out.

"Hey, Miss Ruby. Off to the art room?" I asked as I held the doors open.

"Yeah. I'm meeting my new friend, Isabelle, there. Oh shoot, I forgot my special paint brush. I have to go back upstairs."

She stepped back inside and I pushed the button to the twenty-second floor as well as the twenty-fifth. The doors closed and we made it up between the ninth and tenth floor when the elevator lurched, and we came to a complete stop.

"Shit."

"Nathan, what happened? Why aren't we moving?"

"It seems that the elevator may have gotten stuck in between floors," I spoke as I pushed the emergency button.

"Really? Super cool. I've never been stuck in an elevator before." She grinned.

"Well I have, and it's no picnic."

I pulled my phone from my pocket with the hopes that I had some sort of service and let out a sigh when I found that I didn't.

"I need you to stay calm, Ruby. I'm sure it'll get moving in a few minutes."

"I'm calm. I can't wait to tell Isabelle how I got stuck," she spoke with excitement. "Hey, Nathan?"

"Yeah." I glanced down at her. "Are you a pilot?"

"I am." I smiled.

"I could tell by your uniform. Did you just get back from work?"

"I did. I was gone for four days."

"I wondered why I hadn't seen you around." She smiled as she took a seat on the ground. "That is so cool."

"Do you mind if I sit down next to you?" I asked.

"Nope. Not at all. Have a seat." She patted the ground.

I sat down and sighed. It was a damn good thing I wasn't claustrophobic.

"How's your mom doing?" I asked out of curiosity.

"She's okay. I met your brother Elijah a couple of days ago."

"You did? Where at?"

"At the office. My grandma took me there so we could pick my mom up for lunch. And I met your mom and Aspen."

"You've pretty much met my whole family." I smiled. "The only one left is my little brother, Mason."

"Yeah, and they're all super nice. Elijah is funny."

I furrowed my brows at her in confusion.

"I'm happy you like my family. So, you made a new friend?"

"Yeah. She just moved in with her parents. They live in apartment 1610, so you can cross Mr. and Mrs. Hammond off your list and add her family."

"Where did Mr. and Mrs. Hammond go?"

"Mr. Vincent told me that they decided to move to Vermont to be closer to their grandchildren."

"Ah. I see."

"Nathan?"

"Yes, Miss Ruby?"

"I'm getting a little freaked out now. It seems like it's been a while."

"Don't be freaked out, kid. They'll get us moving soon."

"I hope so. I want my mom."

I glanced over and saw the worry on her face, so I started singing.

"Here comes the sun. Do do do do. Here comes the sun."

"And I say, it's all right." She smiled as she sang the words.

"You know that song?"

"Are you kidding me?" Her face lit up. "That's one of my favorite songs by The Beatles."

"Shut up! You like The Beatles?"

"I love them."

"Me too. They're my favorite band of all time." I held my fist out to her for a fist bump.

"Mine too."

"Shall we start over?" I gave her a smirk. "You first, my lady."

She sang the first verse, I sang the second, and we continued until we reached the end of the song. We made it through three songs when suddenly, the elevator started going up.

"Yes! We're moving," Ruby spoke with excitement.

"See, that wasn't so bad, was it?"

When the doors opened to her floor, I saw Allison standing there.

"Thank God, Ruby." She bent down and hugged her tight. "Are you okay? You must have been so scared."

"I'm fine, Mom. I had Nathan to keep me company. We sang some Beatles songs."

Allison stood up and stared at me as I held the door open.

"Thank you, Nathan."

"No problem, Allison. I'll see you around."

Just as I moved my hand and the doors started to shut, I heard Ruby call my name.

"Nathan!"

"Yes." I stopped the door from closing.

"I like you and I'm happy we got stuck together."

"Thanks, kid. I like you too. Go get your favorite paint brush and paint some beautiful pictures." I winked at her before the door closed.

CHAPTER 19

*A*llison

The moment the door to the elevator opened and I saw Nathan standing there with Ruby, I was in shock. When he was in his pilot's uniform, he took sexy to a whole new level. Damn.

"Mom, did you know that The Beatles is Nathan's favorite band too?"

"No, sweetie, I didn't." I took hold of her hand as we walked to our apartment.

"We sang Here Comes The Sun, Hello, Goodbye and Ob-La-Di Ob-La-Da. It was so much fun!"

"That's great. I'm happy Nathan was with you to keep you entertained. Now go get your paint brush and I'll take you down to the art room. But you have to be back in a couple of hours. Grandma and Grandpa are coming over for dinner."

"Yay!"

A couple hours later, I headed to the elevator to go and get Ruby from the art room. I couldn't stop thinking about how she could have been in that elevator alone when it got stuck. When the doors opened to my floor, I saw Nathan standing there in a pair of black dress pants and a gray button-down shirt with the sleeves slightly rolled up. The scent of his cologne not only smacked me in the face, it aroused me.

"Hello, there." He grinned as I stepped inside.

"Hey. You look nice."

"Thank you. I have a dinner date. You see, there are women out there who would love to have dinner with me."

"I'm sure there are." I pursed my lips.

When the doors opened to the lobby, I stepped out first.

"Have fun on your date," I spoke as I walked away.

"I fully intend to. Thank you."

I rolled my eyes as I lightly shook my head on my way to the art room.

"Look what I painted, Mom." Ruby held up a picture of painted trees and sunflowers.

"Ruby, that's beautiful. You get your artistic talent from your dad. We'll find the perfect spot to hang it up when we get upstairs."

"I painted it for Nathan," she spoke.

"Oh. I'm sure he'll love it."

"Can we run up to his apartment so I can give it to him? Please, Mom."

"Not tonight, sweetie. Nathan isn't home. He went out."

"How do you know?"

"I ran into him in the elevator on the way down to get you."

"Oh." She looked down in disappointment.

"You can give it to him tomorrow." I patted her head.

☙

While my dad was in Ruby's bedroom reading her a bedtime story, my mom helped me clean up the kitchen from dinner.

"So, who is this Nathan guy that Ruby keeps talking about?" she asked.

"He lives in the building. He's actually Elijah's brother."

"Really?" She smiled. "Is he just as handsome?"

"Yeah. He's handsome," I replied as I dried the pan she just washed.

"Is he single?"

"Yes, Mom, he's single."

"What does he do for work?"

"He's a pilot."

"Wow. Single, handsome, a Wolfe, and a pilot. He sounds like the perfect package."

"Stop, Mom." I shot her a look.

"Stop what, darling?"

"I know what you're doing. I'm not interested in him. He's—he's—he's a total womanizer. He has women all over the country he visits on his layovers and he's—he's—"

"He's what, darling? The way you're getting all worked up by talking about him sounds to me like there might be a little bit of interest there."

"There is absolutely no interest on my part for Nathan Wolfe. He's not my type. He's not—"

"He's not Jared? Of course he's not, Allison. There will never be anyone like Jared, but that doesn't mean there isn't anyone else out there who's not worthy of your love and your time."

"Just stop." I sighed.

"Listen, darling." She placed her hand on my shoulder. "I worry about you every day. You're far too young just to give up. Plus, you need to have sex sometimes."

"Oh my God, Mom. I can't believe you just said that!"

"Well, it's true." Her brow arched.

"My husband has been dead for a year. Only one year and you want me to run out and find someone to have sex with?" I voiced rather loudly.

"What is going on out here?" my dad asked. "Ruby just fell asleep."

"Mom is telling me I need to start dating and have sex."

"Carol, really?"

"All I said was she's too young to give up."

"Allison will make that decision when she's ready and when the time is right." He kissed my forehead.

After they left, I went into the bathroom and started the bath. As I stared at myself in the mirror while I twisted my hair up, tears sprang to my eyes. I took in a deep breath and climbed in the tub. Reaching for my phone, I decided to text Nathan. I knew he was on a date, but I didn't care.

"*Hi. Ruby painted a picture for you today and she wanted to give it to you, but I told her you weren't home. So, I said she can give it to you tomorrow.*"

"*That was nice of her. Of course she can give it to me tomorrow.*"

CHAPTER 20

Nathan

"Who are you texting?" Elijah asked as we sat at the table at Rudy's kicking back a few drinks.

"Just a friend of mine." I lied.

Mason looked at me with a narrowed eye for he knew I was never so vague with my answers.

"Aspen is calling. I'll be right back," Elijah spoke as he got up from the table to find a quieter spot to talk.

"You were texting Allison, weren't you?" Mason asked.

"She texted me first. I ran into her on the elevator, and I may have told her I was going on a date." I smirked. "Apparently, Ruby painted me a picture and wants to give it to me."

Mason chuckled. "Wow. Seems like your plan is working."

"I haven't had the chance to implement it yet since I've been working. But it's obvious my charm worked on her when we were stuck in the elevator."

"Look at you, Daddy Nathan." He smirked.

"Shut your mouth." I pointed my finger at him.

"Why are you telling him to shut his mouth?" Elijah asked as he took his seat.

"It's nothing. He's just being his usual douchebag self. Anyway, your big bachelor party is next weekend." I grinned. "Are you ready for some wild and crazy Vegas fun?"

"Can't wait."

"And Aspen is okay with this?" Mason asked.

"Of course she is. She trusts me. But I am a little worried about her bachelorette party."

"Why?" I furrowed my brows at him.

"Because Mom is in charge," he spoke as he picked up his drink.

"God knows what she's going to do." I shook my head.

"Where is the party at?" Mason asked.

"I don't know. She won't tell anyone yet. Not even Aspen, which worries me."

"Yeah. I'd be a little worried too." I finished off my drink.

※

The next morning, I stumbled out of bed, took a shower and made a cup of much needed coffee. Today was Labor Day and my mom was hosting our annual family picnic at Central Park. Picking up my phone, I sent Allison a text message.

"Good morning. If you're home, I can run down and pick up that picture Ruby made for me."

"Morning. We're here. Stop by whenever you want."

"Great. I have to run out for a few. I'll stop up on my way back."

"Sounds good."

I finished my coffee, popped two aspirin and headed down the street to the bakery to pick up some donuts for Ruby as a thank you for the picture. I deemed it appropriate for my plan, and what child doesn't like donuts?

Holding the white box in my hand, I knocked on the door. As soon as it opened, Ruby stood there with a wide grin on her face.

"Nathan, you're here! I made you something."

"I know. Your mom sent me a text message last night and told me.

I have something for you too." I opened the box and showed her the variety of donuts.

"I love donuts! Come in. Mom, Nathan's here and he brought donuts!" she yelled.

"He did," she spoke as she came from the hallway.

"I'll be right back. I'm going to get the picture I painted."

"Hi, Nathan," Allison said.

"Hi, Allison."

"How did your date go last night?"

"It went great. Thanks for asking." I lied.

Ruby ran back into the room and handed me the picture she painted.

"Here."

"Wow, kid. This is beautiful. You really painted this for me?"

"Yes. I hope you like the sunflowers."

"I do. They're beautiful. Thanks." I patted her on the head with a smile.

"Would you like some coffee to go with your donut?" she asked.

"I really can't stay."

"Please, Nathan," she whined. "Please sit and have a donut with us. Please."

I looked over at Allison as she stood there with a smirk on her face.

"You know what? I have some time. A cup of coffee sounds great."

"Yay! I'll make you some."

"I'll make the coffee, Ruby. You and Nathan go sit at the table."

"Which donut do you want?" Ruby asked as she opened the box.

"You pick first. I bought them for you." I smiled.

"I want the pink one with sprinkles."

"Excellent choice."

Allison set my mug down in front of me and I picked it up and took a sip. Sitting down in the chair across from me, she picked up a donut from the box and looked at it.

"That one is custard filled," I said.

"Oh. My favorite." The corners of her mouth curved upward.

"Mine too." I picked the other one from the box.

I wouldn't lie and say this wasn't awkward, because it was. Me, of all people, sitting at a table sharing donuts with a woman I was interested in and her kid. But, as far as I was concerned, today was the perfect day to try and get to know her a little better. I knew if I asked her what I was about to in front of Ruby, she'd have no choice but to agree.

"So, are the two of you doing anything for Labor Day?"

"Not really. I was going to take Ruby to Central Park later for a picnic."

"Your family isn't doing anything?" I asked.

"My parents are meeting some friends at the country club and my brother is going to his in-laws for a barbeque."

"Well then, you're in luck." I grinned. "My mother is having her annual Labor Day picnic at Central Park at two o'clock. Everyone in the family will be there. Join us."

"Can we, Mom?" Ruby asked with excitement in her voice.

"Thanks for the offer, Nathan, but I don't think so."

"Mom," Ruby whined.

"Why not? It'll be fun. We do this big barbecue with hot dogs and hamburgers. We play a little frisbee and some football. You said you were going to take Ruby to Central Park anyway, so join us. My mom and Elijah will be thrilled."

"Mom, please. It'll be so much fun. It'll take my mind off having to go back to school tomorrow. Please, Mom. Please."

Allison stared at her for a few moments, and I could see the hesitation splayed across her face.

"Are you sure it'll be okay with your mom?"

"If it'll make you feel better, I'll ask her now." I pulled out my phone and sent her a text message.

Is it okay if Allison and her daughter, Ruby, join us today?

Of course. I'd love to have them there.

"See." I smiled as I held up my phone to show her. "She'd love to have you and Ruby there."

"Okay. We'll go for a little while."

"Yay!" Ruby smiled at me as she held up her hand for a high-five.

"Thanks for the coffee. I better get going. We'll be up on Great Hill at two o'clock. You can't miss the Wolfe family barbeque. My mother has a large area all roped off."

"How does she manage that?" She let out a laugh.

"Have you not met my mother?" I arched my brow at her.

She continued to laugh as I headed towards the door.

"Should I bring something?"

"No. My mother has the entire barbeque catered. She even has people do the barbequing for her. Everything is taken care of."

"Oh. Okay."

"See ya later, Miss Ruby. I'll bring my guitar and we can sing some songs."

"Beatles?" she asked.

"Of course. There's nothing else worth singing, is there?"

"No." She giggled.

CHAPTER 21

*N*athan

When I arrived at the park, everyone was there except Mason.

"Where's Mason?" I asked Elijah as he handed me a beer.

"He'll be here shortly."

"Hi, Nathan." Aspen smiled as she walked up holding Mila.

"Hey, Aspen." I kissed her cheek. "Hello, sweetheart." I kissed Mila's forehead. "I ran into Allison in the building and invited her and Ruby to join us."

"Great." Aspen grinned. "That'll be fun."

Elijah hooked his arm around me.

"Why did you invite one of my associates?"

"Because she mentioned she didn't have plans and so I thought why not. Nobody should have to spend Labor Day alone. Right?"

He glared at me with a narrowed eye.

"I'm sorry. Is it against your rule to have one of your associates attend a family function?" I asked.

"It is if my brother is chasing one of my associates."

"I'm not chasing anyone, Elijah."

"Hello, darling." My mother kissed my cheek. "What's going on over here. I'm sensing tension."

"No tension, Mother. Just catching up with my brother." Elijah smiled as he gripped my shoulder.

"Elijah, can you come over here please," Aspen shouted a few feet away.

"We'll talk about this later," he said as he walked away.

"There's nothing to talk about," I shouted.

"What's going on?" Mason asked as he walked up behind me.

"It's about time you got here. I stopped by Allison's earlier with a box of donuts for Ruby and I invited them to join us today. Elijah doesn't seem happy about it. He thinks I have an ulterior motive."

"You do." He chuckled before sipping his beer.

"And our big brother doesn't need to know that. After today, I know I'll be in the good graces of Allison and with any luck, she'll agree to have dinner with me."

"Just be careful, bro. In the meantime, I'm going to just sit back and watch the show." He patted my back and walked away.

In the distance, I saw Allison and Ruby walking towards our area. Walking over to Aspen, I took Mila from her arms.

"I haven't had a chance to hold my beautiful niece yet." I smiled. "Oh look. Here comes Allison and Ruby."

"Hi, Nathan!" Ruby grinned.

"Hello, Miss Ruby. I would like you to meet, Miss Mila. This is Elijah's and Aspen's daughter." I bent down so she could get a better look.

"She's so cute." She smiled as she touched Mila's hand.

"Hi, Nathan. A baby looks good on you." Allison smirked.

"Thank you. I adore children." I grinned as I felt a light smack on my back. Apparently, Mason heard my comment.

I needed to play it safe as long as Elijah was around. I could feel him watching me, so I stayed away from Allison until the time was right. She mixed and mingled with Aspen and my mother and she appeared to be having a good time.

"Up for a little football before we eat?" I asked as I walked up to my brothers.

"We should ask Tommy," Elijah said.

"Do we have to?"

"We need another person," Mason said.

"I'll go ask him," Elijah spoke as he walked over to him.

I grabbed the football and me and Mason headed to an open spot and started tossing the ball.

"He can't play. He has a bad knee," Elijah said as he walked over to where we stood.

"I heard you guys need another player." Allison smiled as she approached us.

"You play?" I cocked my head at her.

"I used to play with my—my brother and dad."

"Then by all means, show us your skills." I grinned.

"Allison will be on my team," Elijah spoke like the douchebag he was.

He only said that to make sure she wasn't on mine.

"Sounds good to me," I said.

When all was said and done, Elijah and Allison won. But that was only because I couldn't be rough like I usually was. I didn't want to take the risk of hurting her. Elijah on the other hand, suffered a few hard tackles, but he made sure to get back at me for it.

"Boys, it's time to eat," my mother shouted.

"Are you okay?" Allison asked as we walked over to the table. "Elijah tackled you pretty hard."

"I'm fine. He's the one who's hurting." I smirked.

CHAPTER 22

Allison

After we ate, Nathan grabbed his guitar and he and Ruby sat down on the blanket that was spread out. I sat at the table and watched as he strummed, and the two of them began singing. I didn't know exactly how I felt when I watched them. All I knew is that for the first time in a long time, I felt good.

"I didn't know Nathan played the guitar," I spoke to Aspen.

"He's been playing since he was a kid. Mason plays too. I'm surprised he didn't bring his guitar. I hear Mila waking up over there. I'll be right back."

I got up from the bench and walked over to where Nathan and Ruby were.

"Hey, Mom. Sit down and sing with us."

"What are you singing?" I asked as I sat down on the blanket.

"Any song you'd like." Nathan smiled.

"But it has to be a Beatles song," Ruby commanded.

"I have an idea. Let's sing Ob-La-Di Ob-La Da. We'll each take a verse and then sing the chorus at the same time," Nathan spoke. "Do you know the words?" he asked me.

"Yes. I know the words."

"Great. And a one. And a two." He strummed his guitar and sang the first verse, I followed with the second and then Ruby joined in.

※

Elijah

I stood there with my arms folded and watched the three of them singing and laughing.

"They're cute. Aren't they?" Aspen spoke as she wrapped her hand around my arm and laid her head on my shoulder.

"If you're referring to Allison and Ruby, yes. If you're referring to all three of them, no."

"Lighten up, Elijah. Look at them. They're having a great time."

"Nathan is up to something. I can feel it. I know my brother better than anyone else."

"So what. Maybe he does like her and wants to take her out or something. It's really none of your business."

"That's where you're wrong, sweetheart. It is my business when it involves one of my employees. My brother is incapable of having feelings for anyone except his family."

"Sounds like someone else I knew when I first met him. You told me I changed all that for you. Maybe Allison could be the one to change him."

"See, the thing about Nathan is that once he gets what he's after, he's done. He's a very conflicted man and can't sort out his feelings."

"Again, sounds like someone else I knew when I first met him."

I let out a long sigh.

"He's worse than I was, and I will not allow him to use her. Especially after she just lost her husband a year ago. That is one relationship that will not happen."

"You can't help who you fall in love with, Elijah. If Allison was put in Nathan's path for a reason, you nor anyone else isn't going to stop it from happening."

"We'll see about that."

Allison

We sang one more song and laughed our way through it. I was having the best time and somehow, a sense of guilt washed over me.

"It's getting late. We should go."

"No, Mom! I want to stay," Ruby whined.

"Listen, kid, you have a big day tomorrow and you need to get a lot of rest if you're going to blow all those kids out of the water with your smartness. We can do this again. I promise."

"Will you teach me how to play the guitar?"

"Sure. I will."

"Thank you, Nathan." She wrapped her arms around his neck and gave him a hug.

"You're welcome. Have a great first day of school tomorrow."

"I will."

I gave Nathan a smile as I got up and took Ruby by the hand. We said our goodbyes and headed back to the apartment. After she had her bath, I tucked her into bed and kissed her goodnight. Walking into the kitchen to pack her lunch for tomorrow, I poured a glass of wine and there was a knock on the door. Looking out the peephole, I saw Nathan standing there.

"Hi."

"Hi. Ruby left her hat at the park. I just wanted to drop it off, so she didn't think she lost it."

"Thanks." I took it from his hands.

"You're welcome. Enjoy the rest of your night."

He tucked his hands in his pants pockets and began to walk away.

"Nathan?" I called out to him.

"Yeah."

"Would you like to come in for a glass of wine? I just opened a bottle."

"Sure."

What the hell was I doing? The words just fell out of my mouth before my brain could even process what was happening. I grabbed another glass from the cabinet and poured some wine in it.

"Is Ruby sleeping?" he asked.

"Yeah." I handed him his glass.

"Thanks. I hope you and Ruby had fun today."

"We did. Your family is really great. We can go and sit on the couch." I gestured.

"Listen, Allison, I want to apologize again for everything that occurred prior to today. When we first met at the airport and with the lawsuit. And for the record, I think you're a really good mom. Ruby is a great kid. You should be proud."

"Thanks, Nathan. I appreciate it. You know, you don't have to apologize for the lawsuit. I get it. I really do. If I had family who were remarkable and well-known attorney's and they handed my case off to someone new to the firm, I'd feel the same way. But that's all water under the bridge now. I forgive you. Even for your little airport stunt." I smirked. "And as far as Ruby goes, her dad had a lot to do with how she was raised as well."

"Had?" he asked.

I swallowed hard as I looked down at my wine glass.

"My husband passed away a year ago." I choked out the words.

"I'm so sorry, Allison. I had no idea." He placed his hand on my arm.

"Thank you."

"Was it an accident?"

"No. He was out one afternoon on his break at the hospital playing basketball with some of the other residents, and he had a massive heart attack. He was gone in seconds. They did everything they could to try and bring him back, but they couldn't."

"Jesus. I'm sorry. Was he a doctor or something?"

"He was a surgical resident at Northwestern Memorial. He was in his last year. That's why we moved to Chicago so he could finish up his residency."

"How old was he?"

He was twenty-nine." I took a sip of my wine. "I wanted to move back to New York as soon as it happened, but I was in a contract at my previous law firm, Ruby was in school, and I just didn't want to do anything on impulse. So, as soon as Ruby finished school and my contract with the law firm was fulfilled, I packed us up and moved back here to be closer to my family. Not only did I need them, but Ruby did too."

"Well, you did the right thing by moving back. Ruby seems to have adjusted."

"She's doing okay. She's a strong little girl. I honestly don't know how I would have survived if it wasn't for her. She's the one thing that kept me going after Jared's death. I think I need some more wine. Would you like some more?"

"No. It's late and I better get going. You have a big day tomorrow between Ruby's first day of school and work."

"Yeah. You're right. Thanks again for bringing Ruby's hat by."

"You're welcome."

I opened the door, and as he began to walk out, he stopped and turned around.

"I know you said no before, but I still would like to take you to dinner as a thank you for what you did with regards to the lawsuit."

"You're not going to give that up, are you?" I gave him a smirk.

"No. I'm not." The corners of his mouth curved upward.

"Then fine. Just to shut you up, I'll have dinner with you."

"Excellent. Is there a certain night that works for you?"

"Wednesday night would work. My parents are picking Ruby up for their weekly granddaughter dinner."

"Wednesday is good for me too. I'll pick you up around six-thirty. Is that a good time?"

"Six-thirty is great. I'll see you then."

CHAPTER 23

*N*athan

The thought that she'd been married, and her husband passed away never crossed my mind. I was shocked to say the least. I just assumed the guy wanted nothing to do with her or Ruby. Shit. My plan had just gotten a lot trickier. I was sure she hadn't had sex since her husband and if that was the case, this was going to be harder than I anticipated.

I was up by six a.m., threw on a pair of sweatpants and a t-shirt and headed to the gym to meet my brothers for an early morning workout. By time I got there, Elijah and Mason were already at the weight bench. I grabbed a plate on my way over and started warming up.

"It's about time," Elijah spoke.

"I was pretty much up all night."

"Why? Did you go out last night after you left the park?" he asked.

"No. I went home. I just couldn't sleep."

I glanced over at Mason who was staring at me with that "I know you're lying" look on his face. Walking over to the rack, I grabbed two sixty-pound dumbbells and began doing bicep curls.

"Not working chest today?" Mason asked as he laid down on the bench.

"Nah. It's been a while since I did some biceps."

"Allison seemed to have had a good time yesterday," Elijah said.

"Yeah. I guess."

"Her daughter is adorable."

"Yeah. She's a cute kid."

"I don't know if Allison told you, but her husband passed away last year," Elijah spoke.

"What?" Mason said in shock as he finished his presses and sat up and looked at me.

"I didn't know. That sucks." I continued with my set.

"Yeah it does. I know it was really hard on her and still is."

"Okay, Elijah." I set down my weights and looked at him. "What exactly is going on here?"

"Nothing. It's just from what I saw yesterday, it seems like the two of you are very friendly and I don't want to see her get used or hurt."

"Of course me and Allison are friendly. Have you forgotten that she handled my case? The one you gave her because you took off for Florida. So, yes, Elijah, we're friends and that's all."

"And you have no interest in sleeping with her whatsoever?" His eye steadily narrowed at me. "Because she's an incredibly attractive woman and I know you."

"No. She lives in my building. That would be awkward."

"Didn't stop you from sleeping with that Bridgette chick two doors down from you." Mason grinned and I smacked him upside the head.

"Ouch, bro. Come on. What was that for?"

"Bridgette also didn't have a kid."

"Okay." Elijah nodded his head. "I have to get to the office. I'll talk to you both later."

As soon as he walked away, I let out a sigh.

"I can't believe that Allison was married, and her husband died," Mason spoke. "Damn."

"Yeah. I know. She told me last night. I stopped by her place to drop off Ruby's hat she left at the park. She asked me to stay for a glass of wine and I did. That's when she told me."

"And that's why you were up all night? You were with her?"

"No, bro. I just couldn't sleep. She agreed to have dinner with me tomorrow night."

"So you're still going through with your plan?"

"You know me, I don't give up that easily. Regardless of what happened to her husband, I'm still curious about her. It just might take a little more time and charm than I originally planned."

*

I spent the day running some errands and as I walked into my building, I heard someone call my name.

"Hi, Nathan!"

Turning around, I saw Ruby holding the hand of an older woman.

"Miss Ruby." I smiled. "How was your day at school?"

"It was fun. Nathan, this is my Grandma Carol. Grandma, this is Nathan. He lives on the twenty-fifth floor. He's the one I painted the picture for."

"Well hello there, Nathan." She smiled as she extended her hand. "It's very nice to finally meet you."

"The pleasure is all mine, Carol." I smiled back as I placed my hand in hers.

The elevator doors opened and the three of us stepped inside.

"You're not working today?" Ruby asked.

"Nah, I have a few days off. One of the perks of being a pilot." I winked at her and she smiled.

The elevator stopped on her floor and the doors opened.

"Bye, Nathan." Ruby waved.

"Bye, Ruby. It was nice to meet you, Carol."

"And you as well." She slyly smiled as she looked me up and down.

*

Allison

When I opened the door to my apartment, the smell of my mother's homemade chicken soup surrounded me.

"Hey, Mom. You didn't have to cook dinner."

"Hello, darling. Ruby asked if I could make her some soup." She smiled.

"Where is Ruby?"

"She's down in the art room with that little friend of hers. I told her to be back by seven."

"Oh. Okay."

"I met a friend of yours today," my mom spoke as she stirred the soup.

"You did? Who?" I asked as I grabbed a wine glass.

"A tall and brutally handsome man named Nathan."

"Oh. Really?" I poured some wine into my glass.

"I met him when I was bringing Ruby home from school. He seems like a nice man. He was very polite."

"Yeah. He's nice," I spoke as I brought the glass up to my lips.

"You told me he was cute, Allison. That man isn't cute. He's beyond sexy as sin."

"Mom, stop it!"

Damn it. I had to tell her I was having dinner with him tomorrow night because I needed her to watch Ruby for me after they had their dinner.

"I'm having dinner with him tomorrow. Could you and Dad stay with Ruby until I get back?"

"Say what? My daughter is having dinner with a man?" She smirked.

"Stop." I put my hand up. "It's just a friendly thank you dinner. That's all."

"A thank you for what?"

"I handled a small case for him. Elijah was out of town, so he asked me to help out. It was no big deal."

"If you say so. And yes, your father and I would be happy to stay with Ruby after dinner."

"Thanks, Mom." I kissed her cheek.

CHAPTER 24

Nathan

Instead of taking Allison to a fancy restaurant, I chose to bring in the chef my mother used at times, Roberto, to cook a gourmet meal for us. I felt having dinner on my terrace was more intimate and quieter for us to get to know each other better. Would she feel the same way? I wasn't sure. My guess would be no, but I was taking my chances anyway. Plus, I wasn't sure if she was going to be pressed for time because of Ruby. It would be more convenient to have dinner at my place if that was the case.

Knocking on the door of her apartment, I nearly lost my breath when she opened it and I saw her standing there in a short floral black and white sundress with her hair in loose curls that flowed over her shoulders.

"Hi." Her lips gave way to a beautiful smile.

"Hi." The corners of my mouth curved upward. "Wow. You look beautiful."

"Thank you."

"Are you ready to go?"

"I am."

The moment we approached the elevator, the doors opened, and Mr. & Mrs. Lenox stepped out.

"Good evening, Nathan. How are you?" Mr. Lenox asked.

"I'm good, George. You're looking very lovely, Bianca."

"Thank you, Nathan. You're such a sweet boy. Who is this gorgeous woman with you?"

"This is Allison Price. She lives in apartment 2210. Allison, meet George and Bianca Lenox."

"It's very nice to meet you both." She smiled.

"It's our pleasure, my dear," George spoke. "We better get going. We don't want to keep Bob and Anna waiting. You two have a nice evening."

"And you as well." I gave them a nod.

The moment we stepped into the elevator, I pushed the button to the twenty-fifth floor and nervously waited for Allison to ask what I was doing.

"Why are we going up? Did you forget something?" she asked.

"I'll explain when we get to my place."

I opened the door to my apartment and the aroma of fine cuisine infiltrated the air around us.

"Welcome to Casa Wolfe. Fine dining at its best." I grinned. "I have reserved the best table in the place, and I hope it meets your expectations."

"What?" She laughed.

I took hold of her hand and led her to the round table covered with white linen that sat on my terrace. Pulling out her chair, she gracefully took her seat.

"We're having dinner here?"

"Let me explain my reasoning for this. I wasn't sure if you were going to be pressed for time because of Ruby. So, I thought it would be best to skip the crowded restaurants and have a quiet dinner here close to home. That way when you need to leave, all you have to do is step on the elevator."

"That was very sweet of you. Wow, this view is amazing."

Roberto poured us each a glass of chardonnay and told us dinner would be served shortly.

"I take it he's the chef?"

"Yes. He cooks for my mother periodically. Great guy and a wonderful chef. I know you won't be disappointed."

So, Mr. Wolfe. Tell me about you." She picked up the glass and brought it up to her lips.

"Well," I wrapped my hand around my glass, "you know my family already. What you may not know is that my father left us when I was two years old. Elijah was four and Mason had just been born. He told my mother that he couldn't do the father thing anymore and he wanted more out of life."

"That's terrible."

"Yeah. Father of the year."

"So you never knew him?"

"No. Once he left, he never looked back." I took a sip of my wine as Roberto set down our plates in front of us.

"I'm sorry."

"Don't be. A man who could walk out on his wife and children and forget they ever existed isn't worthy of knowing us."

"Your mom and Elijah are both lawyers. When did you decide you wanted to become a pilot?"

"The first memory I have was when I was five years old and my mother took us on a trip to Hawaii. I remember sitting in the airport and looking out at all the planes that were parked at the gates. Instantly, I fell in love with planes. It had become somewhat of an obsession. I loved the idea that a plane could transport you into a whole new realm of different worlds. Different types of foods, sounds, people, languages. My bedroom quickly became filled with everything aviation, including numerous model airplanes and books about flying took up my entire bookcase. My mother brought in a painter and had my ceiling painted with clouds and stars. And then she had different small planes hanging from the ceiling. I would lay in bed at night and just stare up at them and fantasize about flying. The thing that excited me the most was the thought that I never had to be tied down to one place very long. When I was fourteen, our housekeeper's husband was an ex pilot who fixed planes. She introduced me to him, and he taught me how to fly. When I turned sixteen, I flew my first solo plane. When I was seventeen, I got my private pilot's license and when I was eighteen, I obtained my commercial pilot certificate. When I was twenty-one, I started working for the airlines, and got promoted to Captain when I was twenty-nine."

"Wow. It seems like flying is your life?"

"It is. I can't imagine my life without it." I smiled. "Just like Elijah can't imagine a life without the law and Mason can't imagine a life without fires."

"All three of you seem very close."

"We are. We're as tight as brothers can be. Don't get me wrong, we do have our differences at times, and we like to fight. But at the end of the day, we'll always have each other's backs no matter what. You know, I admire you."

"You do? Why?" She cocked her head with a light smile.

"Because you went to college and law school while you had a kid. Not many people can do that."

"I have a great family. Ruby wasn't planned, and when I found out I was pregnant, it really hit us hard. I was ready to give up college so Jared could finish his degree. But my parents wouldn't hear of it. Before I had Ruby, Jared and I got married. It wasn't a big wedding or anything. It was done at the courthouse. After that, my father put us up in an apartment and helped us out financially and with Ruby. It was hard but we did it, and I don't have one regret. Speaking of family, my mom mentioned that she met you."

"Yes, we met. Your mother is an attractive woman. I see where you get your looks from." I gave her a wink.

CHAPTER 25

Allison

"Thanks." I could feel the heat rising in my cheeks. "By the way, did you know that your mother is my father's attorney?"

"Say what? No. I didn't know that."

"That's how I got the interview at Wolfe & Associates. My father mentioned I was a lawyer and your mother had an opening at the firm."

"That's great. I'm happy it worked out the way it did. Want to hear something really weird?"

"Sure." I smiled.

"Aspen's father and my mother had carried on a secret relationship for years and no one ever knew. That's how Aspen got hired shortly after her father passed away. Boy, when she found out, it was a shit show. And on Thanksgiving too. Eventually they talked it out and all is good."

"How did she find out?"

"I was looking for a deck of cards because we were all going to play poker and I found a picture of my mother and some guy hidden in the cabinet. When I pulled it out, Aspen walked over and saw it. That's when everything exploded."

"Wow. I'm not sure I would have wanted to be there."

"I didn't even want to be there after that. Aspen said some things to my mother, ran out of the house in tears, Elijah ran after her and the rest is history."

As I sat there and listened to him, I knew the only reason he planned this dinner for us at his place was because it was close to his bedroom. I wasn't stupid and he knew it. But yet, he didn't care. I did believe though there was some truth to what he said about being pressed for time because of Ruby. Like I'd said before, I always knew when people were lying.

"Can I ask you something, Nathan?"

"Of course, love. You can ask me anything you'd like."

"You wanted to have dinner here because you were under the impression we were going to have sex. Am I right?"

"Allison, I would never."

I sat there and narrowed my eye at him as he poured me another glass of chardonnay.

"You're lying. There's one thing you should know about me and that is I know when people lie. I know when my clients are lying to me, the opposing attorney, witnesses, friends, everyone. So just come clean."

He took in a sharp breath as he picked up his glass.

"Fine. Is it so wrong that I want to have sex with you and have wanted it since the first day I laid eyes on you? Is it so wrong that I find you incredibly sexy and I can't stop thinking about it?"

"I'm flattered, Nathan. I really am. But my wound is still fresh and open, and I just can't. But I like you as a friend and Ruby adores you, and we want you in our lives, as our friend."

He sat across from me slowly nodding his head.

"Okay, Allison. I completely understand, and I like you and Ruby as well. So friends it is." He extended his hand to me from across the table.

"Thank you for understanding. If the circumstances were different." I softly placed my hand in his.

"I get it. I really do, and I'm sorry for your loss. As your friend, I'm always here if you want to talk."

I gave him a small smile as I placed my napkin on the table.

"I should get going. It's getting late and I'm sure my mom and dad want to get home."

"Yes. Of course." He got up from his seat.

"Thank you again for a wonderful dinner. I really enjoyed it." I softly kissed his cheek.

"You're welcome, Allison. I'll see you around. If you ever need anything, give me a call."

"I will. Goodnight, Nathan."

"Goodnight, Allison."

I shut the door behind me and let out a deep breath. If only the circumstances were different.

※

"Well, how was your date?" My mom asked with a wide grin as I stepped through the door.

"It wasn't a date, Mom. It was a thank you dinner between a client and his attorney."

"And where did Nathan take you for dinner?"

"He brought in a chef up to his apartment and we had dinner on his terrace."

"Sounds like a date to me, sweetheart." My dad smirked.

"It wasn't. He told me he did it in case I was pressed for time having to get home for Ruby."

"Alright, dear. Keep telling yourself that." She kissed my cheek. "I'll see you tomorrow when you get home from work."

"Thanks, Mom. Thanks, Dad."

"It was our pleasure, princess," my dad spoke as he kissed my forehead.

As soon as they left, I went into the bathroom and started the water for a bath. After pouring in some rose scented bubble bath, I climbed in and lay there as I thought about Jared. Tears started to stream down my face like they did every night. I missed him so much and the life we had. But I knew deep down in the core of my soul that I had to move on at some point because he was never coming back.

CHAPTER 26

Nathan

I stood there with my hands tucked into my pockets as the door shut. Sighing, I walked over to my bar and poured myself a scotch, downing it in one gulp. This was not how I planned the evening would go. She showed me tonight that she was a wounded bird unable to move on. Grabbing my phone, I sent a text message to Mason.

"Can you meet me at Rudy's?"
"Your dinner date is over already?"
"Unfortunately."
"I'll be there in fifteen."
"Thanks."

I arrived at Rudy's before my brother did, so I took a seat at the bar.

"Hey, Nathan. Usual?"

"Hey, Hanna. Yeah and make it a double. Pour Mason one as well. He'll be here soon."

"Coming right up."

As soon as Hanna set the drink down in front of me, I felt a hand on my back.

"What's going on? Why did your date end so early?" Mason asked as he took a seat on the stool next to me.

"Hey, Mason." Hanna smiled at him.

"Hey, Hanna. Thanks." He smiled back as he picked up his glass.

"Allison called me out. She asked me if I arranged dinner at my place thinking she'd have sex with me. Then she went on about how she knows when people lie to her and told me to come clean."

"Damn, bro. What did you say?"

"I told her the truth and she said that she likes me as a friend. Do you believe that? Women don't want to be friends with me. They want way more. With the exception of a couple of them around the world."

"Friends have sex," he spoke. "It's not like you want a relationship with her or anything."

"She said if the circumstances were different. But her wound is still fresh and open, and she can't." I rolled my eyes.

"Bro, put yourself in her shoes. Men are different. We want sex all the time. We don't get emotionally invested like women do. She's still not over her husband's death and it may take her years before she is. My advice to you is to forget about Allison. Yeah, she's hot and a great woman, but you're just wasting your time chasing her. Listen, we leave for Vegas Friday morning. You can have all the sex you want there. We all can. Well, not Elijah of course. But we have nobody stopping the two of us from having the time of our lives." He patted my back.

"You're right, brother. Look out Vegas, the Wolfe brothers are coming to town." I grinned at him as I held up my glass.

"Damn right." Mason smiled as he tipped his glass to mine.

Elijah's driver drove the three of us to the hanger where the private jet my mother rented for us sat. We boarded the plane and took our seats.

"This is weird," Mason spoke.

"What is?" Elijah asked.

"This is the first time the three of us are traveling together solo where one of us can't scope out women for sex."

"Damn. I never thought of that," I spoke. "Sucks to be you, Elijah. Are you sure you don't want one last fling before you tie the knot?"

"What the hell is wrong with you? Absolutely not. Aspen is the only woman I want for the rest of my life. But I don't expect the two of you to understand that. Maybe someday you will."

I let out a chuckle. "No offense, bro, but I'm happy being a forever bachelor. I'm not tying myself down to one woman."

"Me either," Mason chimed in.

"Suit yourselves. To be honest, I already miss Aspen and Mila."

"God, Elijah. You're not going to be a Debbie downer on this trip, are you?" I asked.

Suddenly, we heard multiple voices as more people stepped onto the plane. Turning around, my eyes widened when I saw my mother, Aspen, Colleen, Marie and Allison.

"What the hell?" Mason said.

"What is going on?" Elijah asked with a smile as he got up and hugged Aspen.

"Surprise!" my mother spoke. "We're having Aspen's bachelorette party in Vegas!" A wide grin graced her face.

"You're kidding me," I said.

"I knew there was an ulterior motive when she told us she rented us a private jet." Mason sighed.

"Don't worry, boys. We won't cramp your style. We'll be sitting up there, sipping mimosas." My mother smiled.

"Hi Nathan," Allison spoke.

"How long have you known about this?"

"I just found out on the way here. Your mother kept it a secret until this morning. All she told us was that she was taking us away for the weekend, but she wouldn't say where."

"What about Ruby?"

"She's staying with Jared's parents. I better get up there with the girls."

"Yeah. I'll talk to you later."

"This party just got a whole lot better." Elijah grinned.

I rolled my eyes and then whispered in Mason's ear.

"This is totally fucked up. How could Mom do this to us?"

"Are you really surprised, bro? Seriously? You know how unpredictable she is."

"I figured she was taking them to a spa retreat. Not Vegas! How the fuck are we supposed to let loose and enjoy ourselves with our mother hanging around?"

"I'm sure they're staying at a different hotel. There's no way Mom would infringe on her son's bachelor party."

"Really? Do you truly believe that?" I asked.

"Bro, I'm trying to be optimistic. Don't ruin it."

CHAPTER 27

Nathan

We'd finally landed. After grabbing our bags, the three of us headed to the limo that was waiting for us. Thank God there were two limos. One for us and one for the ladies. With them taking a separate limo, that meant they were staying at a different hotel.

"The city of sin." I grinned as the three of us climbed inside.

"I'm going to seduce Aspen all over again," Elijah said. "I'm going to pretend we never met and reenact our amazing night in Hawaii."

Mason and I both rolled our eyes.

"Elijah, this is your bachelor party. You're spending it with us. Besides, I'm sure Mom is going to keep the girls very busy," I said.

"Yeah and they aren't staying at the same hotel as us anyway," Mason spoke.

"Doesn't matter. I'll find her."

I sighed as I silently cursed my mother for doing this.

We arrived at the Bellagio and when we stepped out of the limo, another one pulled up behind us.

"No. No. No." I looked at Mason.

"Shit," he said as the women climbed out.

"Perfect." Elijah smiled as he walked over to Aspen and hugged her.

"Mother, may we have a word with you?" I asked through gritted teeth as I lightly took hold of her arm and led her away from the other girls.

"Of course, darlings. What's wrong?"

"What's wrong? Let us tell you what's wrong with this picture. This is Elijah's bachelor party. How the fuck are we supposed to have a wild time when you brought Aspen here?!"

"Yeah, Mom. You really put a damper on things," Mason said.

"Don't be silly, boys. Go have all the wild fun you want. I know I will, and I won't judge you. Besides, what's the harm? Elijah and Aspen are both happy to be here together. Stop being selfish and think about your brother. I need to get us checked in, and I suggest you do the same." She smirked as she walked away.

"Did she just tell us to stop being selfish?" Mason asked.

"She sure the fuck did." I slowly shook my head.

"Hey," Elijah spoke as he placed his hand on my back. "Let's go get checked in and get this party started. We're all meeting at the pool."

"All of us?" Mason asked.

"Listen, Mom had good intentions and I know you're not happy about it, but I am. I promise that we'll do some things alone. Just the three of us." He smiled as he walked away.

"Well, look at it this way, at least he didn't warn you about Allison," Mason said.

"He doesn't have to warn me. Nothing is happening anyway. I have other women to explore here. She made it clear we were never having sex."

We went up to our suites, got settled, changed into our swimsuits and headed to the pool area. The place was swarming with beautiful women in sexy bikinis. This was my slice of Heaven.

"Boys, over here," my mom shouted as she waved in her bikini. "I've rented us the Chairman's Cabana."

"Is she wearing—" I lowered my Ray-bans.

"Unfortunately," Mason sighed. "There's two lounge chairs available over here. Let them stay there."

"We're good right here, Mom," I shouted.

"Suit yourselves, party poopers."

"Like she can talk," I said.

Mason and I took our seats directly across from the cabana where they were at. After placing our order for the Bellagio Mojitos, I placed my hands behind my head and took in the exquisite views of the young and sexy women with bikinis that barely covered anything.

"Bro, look." Mason hit my arm repeatedly.

"What?"

"Look at Allison over there."

I slightly pulled down my Ray-bans as she stood there in a hot pink bikini that left my imagination running wild and left me completely speechless.

"Damn, she's got a hot body," Mason said.

"Why are you pointing that out to me? Are you trying to make it worse?"

"Sorry, man."

Hot wasn't a strong enough word. I needed to keep my eyes off her and focus on the multiple women here that *would* have sex with me.

CHAPTER 28

Allison

I didn't know we were going to Vegas. All Caitlin told me was to pack a couple of swimsuits and some evening wear. I was in total shock when I stepped on the plane and saw Nathan sitting there. I wondered why he wouldn't come join us in the cabana. Perhaps he felt uncomfortable because of his mother. I couldn't imagine he was happy that she infringed on his party plans for Elijah. Or maybe it was because of what I'd said at dinner the other night.

I couldn't help but stare at his ripped body from across the way. Not to mention the way his hair was perfectly styled and the Ray-bans he wore.

"He's a handsome man, isn't he?" Caitlin walked over to me with a smile on her face.

"Who?" I nervously asked.

"Nathan. I saw you staring at him over there."

"No. I wasn't." I bit down on my bottom lip.

"It's okay, Allison. To be honest, I thought maybe the two of you had gotten together when I saw you at his place that night."

"Caitlin, no." I shook my head. "That was totally just business. Besides, I just haven't been the same since Jared passed away."

"Of course you haven't. Losing the love of your life is hard. It feels like you're carrying around this heavy weight in your chest and in your heart. A weight that you think will be there forever."

"Yes. Exactly."

"But it won't be there forever. Let me ask you something. Do you think Jared would want you to put your life on hold because he passed away?"

"No. He always wanted the best for me, and he always made sure I was happy. But I have zero interest in dating someone again."

"Because you're afraid you'll find and fall in love with someone and then you'll experience a tremendous amount of guilt. Am I right?"

"Perhaps."

"I get that. I really do. Let me give you a little piece of advice. There's absolutely nothing wrong with having a little sex to get you through the day. Nobody says you have to meet someone and fall in love. You're a young and sexy woman. Just have some casual fun now and again. Your body and your mind will thank you." She smirked. "Remember, what happens in Vegas, stays in Vegas."

I couldn't believe my boss was telling me to go have sex with someone. Was she referring to her son? Did Nathan say something to her about our conversation? I knew they were close, but I didn't think he would talk to her about everything.

I took a seat in the lounge chair as I sipped on my margarita. Marie and Colleen, Elijah's and Aspen's secretaries, were on either side of me. My eyes kept diverting across the way to Nathan as two women were over there talking to him and Mason. I noticed the wide grin on his face, and it made me uncomfortable.

"Look at those two over there soaking up all the attention," Marie spoke.

"Yeah. Look at those muscular bodies," Colleen spoke in a daze.

"They're both manwhores," I blurted out. "At least I know Nathan is."

"Trust me," Marie spoke. "Mason isn't any better."

"And who cares if they're manwhores," Colleen said. "I'd still do both of them, and at the same time." She smirked.

Nathan and Mason both got up from their lounge chairs and headed over to the bar.

"Excuse me ladies," I spoke as I got up from my chair.

Walking over to the bar where Nathan and Mason stood, I ordered another margarita.

"Having fun yet?" Nathan asked as his eyes roamed over my bikini clad body.

"Totally. How about you?"

"Of course. I always have fun when I come here. I'm actually going to head up to the suite to shower and change for dinner. Apparently, my mother took it upon herself to make reservations for all of us."

"Yeah. She told me." I looked down and his six pack was staring me in the face.

"I'll talk to you later, friend," he said as he grabbed his drink.

"Yeah. See you around, friend." A small smile crossed my lips.

I sighed as I took my drink back to my chair. As I was sitting there sipping on it, all Colleen kept talking about was sex as hot guys walked past us. I wouldn't lie and say I wasn't horny, because I was. And every time I looked at Nathan, it intensified. For the first time since Jared passed away, I wanted sex. Did I feel guilty for wanting it with someone other than my husband? Yes, of course I did. But he wasn't here anymore, and I couldn't spend the rest of my life sexless, even though that's the way I thought before I met Nathan. And how would I ever know if I was ready if I didn't try? I told Nathan the other night I couldn't sleep with him out of fear because I knew he wanted it and a part of me did too.

It became too real the moment I stepped inside his apartment. The reason I confronted him about it was because I thought if I heard him say yes, I would be appalled. But the opposite happened. It turned me on and freaked me the fuck out, so I had to escape as quickly as possible.

"Screw it," I spoke as I got out of my seat and slipped into my coverall.

"Screw what?" Marie asked as her and Colleen both stared at me.

"I wasn't going to take a nap before dinner, but now I'm really tired between the alcohol and the flight, so I'm going to close my eyes for a bit up in my room. I'll see you two at dinner." I casually smiled.

"Okay. Get a lot of rest because we're going to be out all night. Remember this is the city that never sleeps," Colleen shouted as I walked away.

I didn't know what suite Nathan was in and I couldn't very well ask him in case I chickened out, so I needed to come up with a plan. That's when I saw Mason walking through the lobby.

"Mason!"

"Hey, Allison." He smiled.

"Which suite is Nathan staying in?"

"He's in the one next to mine. Follow me. Is there a reason you're going up there?"

"I forgot to ask him about something for Ruby and I was headed to my room anyway, so I thought I'd stop up and ask him before I forgot again." I lied.

"I see. Okay."

We stepped off the elevator and Mason led me down the hall to Nathan's suite.

"He's in this one." He gave me a playful smirk.

"Thanks."

I stood there for a moment and took in a deep breath before knocking on the door.

"Allison? What are you doing here?"

I gasped and my heart started to rapidly beat as he stood there holding the door open with a towel wrapped around his waist.

"You're not with anyone are you?" I asked as I bit down on my lip.

"No. Come in," he spoke with the gesturing of his hand. "Is everything okay?"

"You told me the other night that if I ever needed anything to call you."

"Yeah. I remember. Is there something you need?"

I inhaled a deep breath before placing my hands on each side of his face and brushing my lips against his.

CHAPTER 29

Nathan

I was unprepared and in shock, to say the least. The silky feel of her lips was everything I'd imagined. I wanted to devour her, but something was holding me back. Pulling back, I stared into her beautiful eyes as my hand rested on her cheek.

"Allison, do you know what you're doing? Or is it the alcohol?"

"I know full well what I'm doing, Nathan," she spoke in a soft voice. "I want this. I want to have sex with you."

"But you said—"

"Forget what I said." She brought her finger up to my lips.

That was all I needed to hear as I grabbed her and smashed my mouth into hers. My cock was already standing at full attention and begging to be taken care of. I took the ties of her coverup, untied them and slipped it off her shoulders as her fingers loosened my towel and it fell to the ground. Picking her up, I carried her to the king size bed and gently lay her down while I stroked the outline of her breasts that were partially hidden by her bikini top. As our lips collided, my hand ran down her torso, feeling the softness of her toned flesh as my fingers pushed their way down her bikini bottoms. A sensual moan escaped her lips the moment I touched her sensitive area, and my desire to be inside her was burning out of control with roaring flames inside me.

As I broke our kiss, my fingers hooked into the sides of her bottoms and slowly pulled them down. Reaching behind her, she untied her bikini top and threw it over the side of the bed. The corners of my mouth curved upward as I stared at the gorgeous naked body lying in front of me. Hovering over her, my tongue circled around her hardened peaks before wrapping my lips around them while my finger plunged inside her. She arched her back in pleasure and her moans heightened as my finger explored the inside of her. My mouth made its way from her breasts down her torso and stopping at her clit as I softly circled it with my tongue. To taste her this way was everything I'd imagine it would be.

"Oh God," she moaned as her hands tangled through my hair.

She was on the brink of an orgasm. I could feel it, and nothing gave me more pleasure than to help her with it. As my mouth continued to devour her, I brought my hands up to each of her breasts and took her hardened peaks between my fingers, softly stroking them as I could feel the wetness pour from her.

"Oh God. Please don't stop," she voiced as her legs tightened and she let out a howl that was sweet music to my ears.

Making my way back up to her, one small kiss at a time, I ran my fingers through her hair as I softly kissed her lips.

"Did you enjoy that?" I whispered in between kisses.

"Yes," she replied with bated breath.

"Good, because the best is yet to come."

Climbing off her, I grabbed a condom from my wallet, tore off the wrapper and rolled it over my throbbing cock. Hovering over her, I brought her arms over her head and held onto her wrists as I stared into her eyes and slowly pushed my way inside her. A deep moan rumbled in my throat as her pussy wrapped around my cock, taking me in inch by inch. I moved in and out of her in a steady rhythm, taking in the sounds of pleasure that escaped both of us. I picked up the pace as did the sounds of our moans. Her body released another orgasm and I had no choice but to come with her as I slowed my thrusts and exploded. Letting go of her wrists, her arms wrapped around me as I collapsed on top of her. I could feel the racing of her heart as it took a minute for us to regain our breath. Rolling off her, I removed the condom and threw it in the trash can next to the bed. She rolled on her side and stared at me with a smile across her lips.

"I hope I met your expectations." I grinned as I softly stroked her hair.

"You did. That was amazing."

Suddenly, there was a knock at the door.

"Nathan, it's me. Open up."

"Shit." I jumped up from the bed. "It's Elijah. I'm sorry, love, but you need to hide in the closet," I said as I grabbed her swimsuit from the floor and threw it at her.

"What?"

"Trust me. Please. I'll get rid of him."

The knocking wouldn't stop as I wrapped the towel around my waist and answered the door.

"For fuck's sake, Elijah. I was in the shower."

"Oh. Sorry. I thought maybe you had someone in here."

"Wish I did to be honest." I smirked. "What's up?"

"Mom is taking the girls out on the town after dinner, so it'll just be the three of us. I thought maybe we could hit the poker tables."

"Excellent idea. We'll do that." I patted him on the back and led him to the door.

"I know you're pissed because Mom brought the girls here. But, bro, I'm happy she did."

"Brother, I'm cool with it. We'll still have our fun. No worries. Okay. Goodbye. I'll see you at dinner." I opened the door.

He looked at me with a narrowed eye.

"What is going on with you? Why are you in such a hurry to have me leave?" he asked as he turned around and walked to the bedroom.

"I have to get ready for dinner. You know Mom will kill me if I'm late." I followed behind him.

"Why isn't the bed made? he asked.

"I took a nap, bro. Jesus Christ. What the fuck is this?"

He looked around and then walked back to the door.

"It's nothing. I'll see you at dinner."

The moment he walked out and the door shut, I let out a sigh of relief.

"What was that all about, Nathan?" Allison asked as she stood in the doorway of the bedroom.

"Listen, Allison," I said as I walked over to her and placed my hand on her cheek. "Elijah can't know what happened here. It has to be our secret."

"Why?" Her brows furrowed.

"Because he has a rule about me and Mason having sex with his employees. He's already threatened me about you, numerous times, and I don't want to cause a rift between us at his bachelor party."

"Okay. I wasn't planning on telling anyone anyway. So, what happened between us is our little secret." She smiled.

"Perfect." I leaned in and kissed her lips. "Are you okay?"

"Yeah. I'm great. I better go and get ready for dinner. I'll see you down there."

"Wait," I said as I opened the door and looked both ways down the hallway making sure nobody was around. "Okay. All clear." I smiled as I kissed her forehead.

CHAPTER 30

Allison

I stepped into my hotel room, shut the door and slid my back all the way down until my butt hit the ground. Bringing my knees up to my chest, I hugged them as I sat there and thought about what I'd done. What we'd done. I gulped as I could still feel the trembling of my skin. Nathan was incredible and now my head was clamored with mixed emotions. Fuck.

After showering and slipping into my evening dress, I met the girls in Caitlin's room, and we headed down to the restaurant for dinner. The guys were already down there waiting and as we approached the table, I nonchalantly took the seat next to Nathan. We ate, drank and then parted ways as Caitlin took us to a club and the guys hit up the poker tables.

It was two a.m. when I had just stepped into my room and my phone dinged. Pulling it from my purse, there was a text message from Nathan.

"Are you alone or are you still partying it up with my mother?"
"I just got back to my room. Heading to bed."
"I like the sound of that. Care for some company?"
"Only if you promise to make it worth my while."

"Love, I promise you won't be disappointed. See you in a few."

"I'll be waiting."

I quickly stripped out of my dress and slipped into the hotel robe that was hanging in the closet. The flutters in my belly went into overdrive the moment I heard a knock at the door. Opening it, Nathan's eyes raked over me from head to toe. He stepped inside and shut the door as his mouth smashed into mine while his hand rested on the nape of my neck. The smell of scotch on his breath was intoxicating as was the taste of his tongue in my mouth. My fingers deftly unbuttoned his casual white shirt as I slipped it off his broad shoulders. After untying my robe and letting it drop to the floor, he picked me up as I wrapped my legs around his waist, and he carried me to bed.

I lay there in his arms with my head against his chest after another round of glorifying sex.

"Your mother is one wild and crazy woman."

"I know and I hope she didn't embarrass you too much."

"Not at all." I smiled as I lifted my head and stared at him. "She's such a flirt. Now I know where you get it from."

"Me? I'm not a flirt at all." A smirk crossed his lips.

"Yes you are." I gently smacked him on the chest.

"Okay. Maybe I am. But I can't help it. I love beautiful women." The back of his hand stroked my cheek.

"Why are you still single?" I blurted out.

"I'm single because I choose to be. It's called freedom, love. I can pick up and go on a moment's notice without having to worry about anyone else. I can go anywhere I want, do whatever I want and who I want." A smirk crossed his lips. When you're in a relationship, all that isn't possible."

"That's true to some extent. But when you fall in love with someone, none of that matters. The only thing you can focus on is that one person and how you're going to build the perfect life with them."

"I hate to break it to you, love, but there's no such thing as perfect. And this fantasy people have about their perfect life aren't living in the reality. Listen, as much as I would like to stay, I better go. I'm sure Elijah will be banging down my door in a few hours and if I'm not there he's going to come looking for me," he spoke as he let go of me and climbed out of bed.

"Sure. I understand," I said as I held the sheet up against me.

He slipped into his clothes, grabbed his shoes and leaned over and kissed my lips.

"Thanks for tonight. I'll see you later." He gave me a wink.

"Sleep well."

"I will now." He grinned as he left the hotel room.

Nathan

As the elevator doors opened on Allison's floor, I saw Mason standing there with some chick.

"Hello there." I grinned as I stepped inside. "And who is this lovely lady?"

"This is Claudette. Claudette, meet my brother Nathan."

"Hello, handsome. Perhaps you'd like to join us." She ran her finger down my shirt.

"Ah, no thanks. He's all yours."

"Where did you just come from?" Mason asked.

"It's a long story and one we will talk about in the morning."

"Okay. Sure."

The elevator doors opened, and Claudette and Mason stepped out first.

"Have fun, you two." I smirked as I opened the door to my suite and stepped inside.

After stripping out of my clothes, I climbed into bed. Placing my arm behind my head, I laid there and thought about the conversation we'd had about relationships. Maybe I shouldn't have been so blunt about it, but it was better she knew exactly where I stood and why.

Not that she'd want anything more than just sex. She'd just lost her husband a year ago and I was sure another relationship was the furthest thing from her mind. I had nothing to worry about.

I had only been asleep for a few hours when the knock on my door jolted me out of bed. Slipping on my pajama bottoms, I opened it to find Mason standing there with two coffees and a brown bag.

"Don't tell me you weren't up yet," he spoke as he stepped inside.

"Of course I wasn't. You saw what time I got in. What the hell are you doing up already?"

"Couldn't sleep. Too much excitement here in the land of Vegas."

"What about Claudette? You kick her out or something already?"

"She left after we had sex. Which was fine with me. I didn't want her to stay anyway. I brought coffee and pastries from the shop downstairs. Sit down and tell me what the fuck happened last night and who you were with."

I grabbed a coffee from the carrier and took it to the table. Mason reached in the bag, handed me an apple fritter and took the seat across from me.

"I slept with Allison yesterday. Twice." I brought the cup up to my lips.

"What?" He shook his head in shock. "How the hell did that happen?"

"I had just gotten out of the shower before dinner and she came to my room and threw herself at me. She said she wanted sex. So, being the gentleman I am, I gave it to her. And then again last night in her room after she got back with the girls."

"Wow. Why the sudden change of heart on her part? That explains why she asked me in the lobby what room you were in. Damn. She told me she forgot to ask you something about Ruby. I didn't think she was coming here to have sex with you after what you told me."

"Honestly, bro. I have no clue what happened or why she changed her mind. I asked her and she just told me to forget what she said and then I took her to bed."

"Well, how was she?"

"Great," I nervously replied.

I got up from the table with the cup in my hand, walked over to the window and stared out into the busy city.

"Why am I sensing something isn't right?" Mason asked.

"Everything was perfect. She was exactly how I imagined she'd be. No big deal. Veni, Vidi, Vici."

"So now what? You better hope Elijah doesn't find out."

"I already talked to her about that and she agreed to keep it a secret. She asked me last night why I was still single, so I had to explain to her my views on relationships and where I stood."

"And what did she say about that?"

"Not much. She just told me that when you fall in love with someone none of that stuff matters."

"Sounds to me like she may be falling for you, bro."

"Nah, I think she realized that a life without sex isn't a life at all. Who knows, maybe being in Vegas made her horny. All I know is I'm not complaining."

"Are you going to have sex with her again when we get back to New York?"

"I don't know. If she wants it, of course. If not, I'm covered." I turned and gave him a smirk.

CHAPTER 31

Allison

I pulled my hair up in a high ponytail and threw my sunglasses on to mask the hangover I was sporting. Yesterday was a full day of partying without the guys. They went off and had their own party. I hadn't seen or heard from Nathan at all. I pulled my phone out several times to text him, but then decided against it. I had hoped that maybe we could've had one last hoorah before we left Vegas. Obviously, he didn't feel the same way, or he had one last Vegas hoorah with someone else.

Stepping off the elevator, I met the girls in the lobby at eight a.m. and we all climbed into the limo and headed to the airport. As much fun as I had, I missed Ruby and couldn't wait to get home to see her.

The plane finally landed, and we were back in New York City. We were all tired including Nathan who chose to sit away from the group and get some sleep for the duration of the flight.

"I called ahead and got a car for me and Allison since we're going to the same building," he said to his mother. "No need for us to keep making different stops. I just want to get home."

"Good idea, darling." She smiled as she placed her hand on his cheek.

We said our goodbyes to everyone and climbed into the back of the car. To be honest, I was surprised he did that since we've barely spoken two words to each other since he left my hotel room the other night.

"Did you have a good time?" he asked.

"I did. But I miss Ruby and I can't wait to see her."

"Understandable."

I wanted so badly to ask him what he did last night, but I couldn't bring myself to. Honestly, I wasn't sure if I wanted to know.

"I'm going to be gone all next week," he said as he glanced at me. "I have a full flight schedule. Tell Ruby as soon as I get back, I'll teach her a few chords on the guitar if she's still interested."

"Sure. I'll tell her. Where are you jet setting off to?" I casually asked.

"My first flight is to Los Angeles and from there I'm heading to London. I'll be there a couple of days to rest and then it's back to Los Angeles and then home the day before Elijah's wedding."

"Do you do a lot of international flights?"

"I do. But I pick and choose where I want to go." A smirk crossed his lips.

"It has to be tough sometimes being a pilot."

"For some pilots it is. For me it's not. I love what I do and like I told you before, it gives me the opportunity not to stay in one place too long."

The car pulled up to the building and we both climbed out as the driver grabbed our luggage. The moment we walked up to the elevator, the doors opened. Stepping inside, Nathan pushed the button to the twenty-second and twenty-fifth floor. As soon as the elevator stopped on my floor and the doors opened, I went to step out and Nathan lightly grabbed hold of my arm.

"I had a good time with you, and I hope things don't get awkward between us," he spoke.

"I had a good time with you too. No awkwardness here." I gave him a soft smile.

"None over here, either. I'll talk to you later."

"Have a safe trip, Nathan."

I opened the door to my apartment and took my suitcase straight into the bedroom. My parents ended up taking Ruby to the Hamptons for the weekend to go on the boat and they weren't dropping her off for another four hours. Just as I laid down on the bed to take a nap, my phone dinged with a text message from my brother Rick.

"Hey, sis. I'm in the neighborhood and wondered if you were home yet?"

"I just walked through the door about ten minutes ago. Come on over."

"Great. I'll be there in five."

As much as I needed a nap, Rick's timing couldn't be better. The fact that I hadn't and couldn't talk to someone about what happened with Nathan was destroying me mentally. I needed to talk to someone about it.

"Good to see you, sis." Rick smiled as he kissed my cheek.

"Good to see you too. Come on in. Coffee?"

"Sure. That'll be great," he spoke as he took a seat at the island. "How was your trip?"

"It was good." I gave him a soft smile. "Exhausting, but good. I really needed that little getaway."

"I agree and I'm happy you decided to go."

I set his coffee cup down in front of him and sighed.

"Something's wrong. I can tell."

"I had sex this weekend." I bashfully turned around and popped another k-cup in the Keurig.

"What? With who?"

I turned and looked at him as I bit down on my bottom lip.

"Nathan Wolfe."

"Allison, seriously?"

"Listen, Rick, don't judge me." After the coffee was done brewing, I grabbed my cup and leaned over the island. "Between the atmosphere, all the excitement, the alcohol and his hot muscular body, I just snapped, went to his suite and practically threw myself at him."

He let out a chuckle as he brought his cup up to his lips.

"So you initiated it?"

"Basically. But he eluded he wanted to have sex with me since the moment we met."

"And?" A sly smile crossed his mouth.

"It was incredible, and it happened twice—in one day."

"How are you feeling about it now?"

I took a sip of my coffee.

"I don't know to be honest. I feel like I'm on a Nathan Wolfe high."

"Do you have feelings for him?"

"I don't think they're real. You know how women are. We tend to attach to the emotional side of sex. He's the first guy I had sex with since Jared and the fact that he wanted me, made me feel good. He made me feel sexy again. So, that's the high I'm on right now." I let out a sigh.

"If you want my opinion, I think you did the right thing. You took the first step towards healing. You opened yourself up to someone else and I think it's great. I probably would have dated someone first before jumping right into bed, but hey, to each his own." He smiled and I lightly smacked his arm. "What I'm actually saying is that the scary part is over."

CHAPTER 32

Nathan

I grabbed my tux and my bag and headed to the limo downstairs where Mason was waiting for me.

"It's about time, bro."

"Considering I didn't get in until midnight after a long work week, you're lucky I even remembered to set my alarm."

"I had a tough week too at the station. It was one damn fire after another."

"I can't believe our brother is getting married today. Who would have thought?" I spoke.

"I know. It's crazy. But him and Aspen are perfect for each other. They're the perfect balance. Don't you think?"

"I guess." I furrowed my brows at him.

"How's Allison doing?" Mason asked.

"I don't know. I haven't seen her all week."

"You didn't text her while you were away?"

"No. Why would I?"

"I just thought maybe with her being one of Elijah's key lawyers, you'd be a little more sensitive. I'm sure she's probably wondering why she hasn't heard from you after you fucked her two times in Vegas."

"To be honest, I don't think she thinks anything. She knows how I am. And besides, I told you what happened between us was just sex and nothing else."

"Yeah. Yeah. I know."

We arrived at my mother's townhome and when we stepped inside, Elijah was walking down the stairs in a pair of gray sweatpants.

"Why aren't you dressed yet?" I asked.

"Because I was waiting on you two douchebags to get here." He smiled as he gave us each a light hug.

"You ready for this, brother?" Mason asked.

"As ready as I'll ever be."

"Where's Mom?" I asked.

"Upstairs with Ricky. He's finishing up her hair and makeup. Let's go and get ready. We have a photoshoot in an hour."

The three of us stood at the bottom of the stairs as my mother walked down in her elegant Valentino dress.

"Wow, Mom. You look gorgeous." I smiled as I kissed her cheek.

"Thank you, darling."

She stood in front of us and I could see the tears filling her eyes.

"Look at you boys. You're all so handsome."

"Mom, don't," Mason said.

Elijah turned away and I knew it was because he was tearing up. *Wuss.*

"Okay. Let's not ruin your makeup before pictures," I said. "Where's Eloise?"

"I'm right here." She grinned as she walked into the foyer. "Hello boys. Caitlin, you look stunning."

"Thank you, darling. And thank you for doing this for me."

"You're welcome. It's my honor to photograph what's going to be the most talked about wedding in New York."

"How's Christian, Eloise?" I asked. "I haven't spoken to him in a while.

"He's good. He said you all have a lot to catch up on later."

After taking some pictures with our mother inside the townhouse, me and my brothers headed to Central Park for a few more.

§▲

Elijah wouldn't pick just one of us to be his best man, so we both were. Since I was the second oldest, I was chosen to stand next to him while Mason stood next to me. As for the ring, both Mason and I would hand it to him together as well as give the speeches at the reception.

The ceremony was about to begin as I glanced over at Elijah and noticed the beads of sweat forming on his forehead.

"Bro, you're not nervous, are you?" I asked.

"About marrying Aspen, no. I'm nervous about getting a boner when I see her coming down that aisle."

"Seriously? Shit." I chuckled.

"Bro." Mason lightly smacked my arm. "Look who just walked in."

I glanced over and saw Allison on the arm of some dude. Instantly, my stomach twisted in a knot. Not just because she looked sexy as hell, but also because she was with someone.

"Who the fuck is that?"

"I don't know. Her date?"

"I've only been gone a week. How the fuck does she have a date already?"

The guy she was with looked like a preppy douchebag as I stared him up and down while they took their seat in one of the pews. I couldn't figure out for the life of me how she met someone so quickly when just over a week ago she wanted nothing to do with guys.

Once the ceremony ended and many tears were shed, we headed to the limo for more pictures in Central Park and then it was off to the Plaza Hotel for the reception. As I was standing at the bar ordering a double scotch, I heard Allison's voice from behind.

"Hey, Nathan. How was your trip?"

"Allison." I turned around and gave her a smile. "It was good. You look stunning."

"Thank you. This is my date, Connor Banes. Connor, Nathan Wolfe."

"Nice to meet you, man." He smiled in his preppy douchebag way as he extended his hand to me.

"Same," I spoke as I shook his hand.

"It was good to see you. We're going to head to our table," Allison spoke. "By the way, Ruby is really excited for those guitar lessons."

"Good." I smiled at her. "We'll have to set something up."

As soon as they walked away, the fake smile I displayed dissipated as I brought my glass up to my lips.

"I saw that," Mason said as he walked up. "Who is that guy?"

"His name is Connor Banes, and she introduced him as her date." I threw the liquid down my throat.

"Wow. She moves just about as fast as you do." He laughed. "Having sex with you must have opened her eyes."

"Shut the fuck up."

"You seem upset, bro."

"Why the hell would I be upset? I could care less what she does or who she sees."

"If you say so," he said and walked away.

My eyes kept diverting over to where Allison and preppy douchebag sat. They were talking, laughing and just overall annoying.

"I see you staring at her." Aspen smirked as she walked up to me.

"Have I told you how beautiful you look." I grinned as I kissed her cheek.

"You have, and I love how quickly you changed the subject."

"I'm just surprised how quickly she met someone. In Vegas, she wasn't seeing anyone at all and a week later, she's bringing someone to the wedding."

"Sounds like you're jealous."

"I don't get jealous because I have no reason to be. There's nothing between me and Allison Price but a friendly association. She's a friend and I look out for my friends. You know that." I smiled.

"I know you do." She placed her hand on my shoulder.

Suddenly, the band called everyone to gather around for Elijah's and Aspen's first dance as husband and wife.

"I better go find my husband." She grinned. "I love the sound of that." Her nose crinkled.

CHAPTER 33

*A*llison

The bridal dance was beautiful, and I wouldn't lie and say it didn't bring a tear to my eye. Connor stood up and held out his hand to me.

"May I have this dance?"

"Of course." I smiled as I placed my hand in his and he led me to the dance floor.

Once the song ended, another one started to play, and Nathan walked over to us.

"Mind if I cut in?" he asked Connor.

"Not at all. I'll see you back at the table, Allison."

I could feel the trembling of my skin as Nathan took hold of my hand and wrapped his arm around my waist.

"Is Elijah going to be okay with us dancing together?" I asked.

"We're friends, and friends dance together. So, how did you meet him?"

"He's a friend."

"A friend you just met or have known?"

"Why are you so interested in him?" A smirk crossed my lips.

"I'm not. I'm just making sure he's not a douchebag."

"He's not. He's a very nice guy whom I've known for years. Honestly, I didn't want to come here alone. It's kind of hard— you know."

"Right. I'm sorry, Allison. I know it's tough on you. All you had to do was ask and I could have been your date." The corners of his mouth curved upward.

"Perhaps I could have but I didn't want you to feel like you had to entertain me with all these beautiful women here you could have your pick from."

"Really?" He cocked his head. "Because the only beautiful woman I see here tonight is you."

I swallowed hard as I stared into his eyes and felt the rapid beating of my heart.

"You were gone an entire week and didn't bother to text me," I said. "If this is about sex again, all you have to do is ask."

"Wait, what? You'd have sex with me tonight if I asked you?"

"Yeah. Actually, I would." My brow raised.

"What about preppy douchebag over there?"

"Connor is a friend and nothing more. I've known him and his husband for years."

"His husband?" His brow arched.

"Yes. His husband."

The song ended and Nathan let go of me.

"I'm staying in Suite 1805 tonight. Would you care to join me later?"

"Ruby is staying with my parents for the night so I would love to join you."

"Hey, you two. What's going on over here?" Elijah asked as he walked over to us.

"Nothing much," I spoke. "I was just asking Nathan how his trip was and telling him how excited Ruby is for her first guitar lesson."

"Ah. I see."

"Anyway, it was nice chatting with you, Nathan. I need to get back to my date."

"And I have all these beautiful women here to hit on." He smirked as he lightly smacked Elijah in the chest and walked away."

I walked back to the table, took my seat and picked up my drink.

"I decided I'm going to stay at the hotel tonight," I spoke as I looked at Connor.

"Ah. Does it have anything to do with that sexy man you were dancing with?" He smirked.

"Maybe." I bashfully smiled.

"You go girl." He nudged my shoulder.

I had a long hard week to think while Nathan was gone, and I came to the conclusion that there was nothing wrong with occasionally having sex with him. I wasn't ready to date yet, and I did have needs like any other woman. There was absolutely nothing wrong with what I was doing. Nothing at all, except we had to keep it a secret from Elijah.

Nathan

I walked up to the bar where Mason stood and ordered another drink.

"I saw you dancing with Allison. How did it go?"

"It went great." I grinned. "She's meeting me up in my suite tonight. Turns out preppy douchebag is her gay married friend she brought because she didn't want to come alone."

"So where is all this going?"

"What do you mean? It's going nowhere. She's no different from all the other women I fuck."

"You sure about that, bro?" He placed his hand on my shoulder and walked away.

I shook my head as I threw back my scotch.

It was after midnight and Elijah and Aspen made their rounds and said goodbye to their guests that were still celebrating.

"Have an amazing honeymoon, bro." I hugged him.

"Thanks, Nathan. Thank you for everything."

"You know I'd do anything to see you happy. Goodbye, Aspen. I'm very proud to have you as my sister-in-law." I wrapped my arms around her and gave her a squeeze.

"Thanks, Nathan. You're too sweet. Don't get into any trouble while we're gone." A smirk crossed her lips before kissing my cheek.

"I wouldn't dream of it." I gave her a wink.

After they left, my mother walked up to me and Mason.

"One down and two to go." She smiled at us.

"Yeah, no thanks, Mom." My brows furrowed.

"Same, Mom. You're just going to have to get used to the fact that your two younger sons will forever be bachelors." Mason hooked his arm around me.

"In all honesty, I can't say I blame you." She kissed both of our cheeks before walking away.

When I glanced over at Allison's table, I noticed her and Connor getting up from their seats and heading towards the door to the lobby. Pulling out my phone, I sent her a text message.

"I'm heading up to my suite now."

I watched as she looked down at her phone.

"I'm walking Connor out and saying goodbye. I'll be up there soon."

Walking into my suite, I took off my bowtie and jacket and threw them on the chair across from the couch. As I was unbuttoning my shirt, there was a light knock on the door. Opening it, I stood there with a smile on my face as my eyes locked with Allison's.

"Can I help you?" I asked.

"I hope you can," she seductively spoke as her hands clasped onto both sides of my opened shirt. "I'm hoping you can give me something." The tip of her tongue lightly swept over her bottom lip causing my cock to rise.

Pulling her in, I shut the door and brushed my lips against hers.

"Trust me, love. I can give you anything you want."

My fingers took down the zipper of her dress as I pushed the fine straps off her shoulders, letting it fall to the ground. I swallowed hard as she stood there braless in a black lace thong and heels. My cock was already throbbing, and we'd barely gotten started.

CHAPTER 34

*A*llison

    Several moans escaped me as he thrust in and out of me at a steady pace. The intoxication I felt wasn't from the alcohol I'd drank, it was from him. It was a different kind of intoxication. One that wouldn't last for a few hours, but for days. The rise was happening as my body contracted and the dreamy high he gave me took over.

"That's it, love. Yes," he moaned as he pushed deep inside and halted, collapsing on top me.

The feel of his warm bated breath against my neck was something to be desired. His heart raced with mine and we both lay still as if we were paralyzed. My nails lightly dug into the flesh of his muscular back while we waited for our bodies to calm. He pulled out of me, removed the condom and threw it in the trash can by the bed. Hooking his arm around me, I snuggled into him and laid my head on his chest.

"It was a beautiful wedding. Don't you think?" I asked as I lightly stroked his chest.

"Yeah. It was great," he replied as he let out a yawn.

"This suite is amazing. Thanks for inviting me up here."

He didn't respond, so I lifted my head and when I looked at him, a small smile fell upon my lips as I saw he was fast asleep.

The next morning, I lay there, turned away from him as his arm was wrapped tightly around me, feeling the soft presses of his lips against my shoulder. Turning around in his arms, a smile graced my face.

"Morning."

"Morning," he spoke. "I'm sorry I fell asleep last night."

"Don't be. You had a very busy and long day. What time is it?" I asked.

"Nine o'clock. How about some room service before we head home?"

"That sounds great. I'm starving."

He reached over to the nightstand and grabbed the room service menu as I sat up and we both looked it over together.

"What sounds good to you?" he asked. "I was thinking the—"

"Eggs benedict," we both spoke at the same time.

The corners of his mouth curved upward. "Excellent choice, love."

He reached for the phone and placed our room service order. When he finished with the call, he placed his hand under the sheet and ran it down my torso.

"We have about thirty minutes until it arrives. Shall we make the most of our time while we wait?"

"Definitely." I grinned as his lips brushed against mine.

After we ate breakfast, I slipped back into my dress from last night and Nathan dressed in his pants and his shirt. Grabbing his suitcoat and bowtie, we left the hotel room and headed to the elevator. When the doors opened on our floor, I gulped when I saw Caitlin standing there.

"Mom!"

"Good morning, you two." She gave us a sly smile.

We both stepped inside and I was humiliated. I felt like a teenager who had just gotten caught by her parents having sex for the first time.

"I didn't know you were staying here last night," Nathan spoke.

"I didn't know you were either, darling. Or you, Allison." The sly smile never left her face.

"Where's Tommy?"

"He's checking us out. I left something in the room and had to go back and get it."

"Did the two of you have fun last night?" she asked as the doors opened and we stepped into the lobby.

"The wedding was beautiful, Caitlin."

"That's not what I'm talking about, dear."

"Mom, stop. Listen to me very carefully," Nathan said as we stood in the middle of the lobby. "You cannot tell Elijah about this. Do you understand me?"

"I know, darling." She brought her hand up to his cheek. "I know how your brother is and I won't say a word about what I saw here today. As long as the two of you had fun that's all that matters. Besides, I can't think of a better woman for you to sleep with." She gave me a wink and I wanted to die. "I better go. Tommy has the car waiting at the curb. I'll talk to you later, Nathan, and I'll see you at the office, tomorrow." She placed her hand on my arm.

"That was awkward," I said after she walked away.

"Very." Nathan shook his head as we walked up to the desk to check out.

Nathan

Busted by my mother. Great. The only good thing was I knew she wouldn't tell Elijah because the last thing she'd want is the two of us fighting. I threw my key to the apartment on the table and went into the bathroom and started the shower. Spending the night with Allison felt right, but the one thing that concerned me was the fact that I didn't want to leave. She had asked if I wanted to come over later to teach Ruby a few chords on the guitar. I told her I would. I didn't have any plans anyway and I didn't want to disappoint the kid.

Later that afternoon, Mason and I met up to return our tuxedos.

"You're never going to believe what happened this morning at the hotel."

"Let me guess. You and Allison had a fight?" He smirked.

"No." I furrowed my brows. "Why would we get into a fight? We aren't dating or anything."

"What happened then?"

"Mom saw us."

"Oh shit!" He laughed. "I didn't know she was staying there last night."

"Neither did I. Imagine my surprise when the elevator door opened and there she was."

"What did she say?"

"Let me tell you. She said she couldn't think of a better woman for me to sleep with."

"She said that in front of Allison?"

"Yes!"

"Oh man." His laughter grew. "You better hope she doesn't mention this to Elijah."

"I already talked to her about it and she said she won't because she knows how he is. Anyway, I have to get going," I said as we walked down the street and I hailed a cab. "I'm going over to Allison's to teach Ruby a few chords on the guitar."

"Ah. Having some family time." He grinned.

"Shut the fuck up, douchebag. I made a promise and I'm going to keep it."

"Have fun, bro." He laughed as I climbed into the cab.

CHAPTER 35

Nathan

"Nathan!" Ruby squealed as she opened the door.

"Hey there, Miss Ruby. Are you ready for your lesson?"

"I am. Come in."

I stepped inside with my guitar and saw Allison standing at the kitchen sink washing some dishes.

"Hey, Allison."

"Hey, Nathan." She smiled. "I ordered us a pizza. It should be here shortly."

"You didn't have to do that."

"Ruby wanted it for dinner since you were coming over." The corners of her mouth curved upward.

"Come on, Nathan." Ruby grabbed my hand and led me to the couch.

I pulled out my guitar, set it on her lap and placed her fingers on the string. The first chord I taught her was the D chord, and I was impressed at how quickly she picked it up. While I was teaching Ruby, Allison sat across from us in the chair and I couldn't help but steal small glances at her while she worked on her laptop.

The pizza arrived and as we were sitting at the table, her phone rang.

"Don't worry about it, Karen. I'll figure something out. You just focus on getting better."

"What's wrong with Miss Karen?" Ruby asked her.

"She's sick with the flu."

"May I ask who Miss Karen is?" I looked at Allison.

"She's my backup for Ruby when my parents and Rick aren't around. Karen was supposed to pick Ruby up from school tomorrow since my parents are leaving for California in the morning and Rick will be at work, and I have to be in court tomorrow afternoon."

"I'll pick her up," I blurted out. "I don't go back to work until Friday."

"Nathan, I couldn't ask—"

"Mom, please." Ruby whined. "That would be so awesome if Nathan picked me up. Please."

"Yeah, Mom. Please." I grinned. "Listen, I'm not doing anything anyway. You're in a bind and friends help each other out."

"Are you sure?"

"Positive. You can pick her up at my place after work."

"Okay. If you insist." She smiled.

"YAY!" Ruby exclaimed as she high fived me.

After we ate, Ruby went to her room to finish her homework and get ready for bed and I helped Allison clean up from dinner.

"Thank you for volunteering to pick Ruby up tomorrow."

"No problem. Like I said, friends help each other out." I placed my hands on her hips and quickly removed them when I heard Ruby coming down the hallway.

"Well, I better get going. Thanks for the pizza, Allison."

"You're welcome."

"I will see you tomorrow after school, Miss Ruby." I tapped her nose.

"Thanks for coming over and teaching me the guitar. It was fun." She grinned. "Can I practice some more tomorrow?"

"You sure can." I smiled as I patted her on the head.

I stood outside the school with my hands tucked into my pants pockets while I waited for Ruby to emerge. Looking around, I was surrounded by Moms who stared at me with devious smiles.

"Hello, there," an attractive older woman approached me. "I haven't seen you around before."

"I'm picking up a friend's daughter. She was in a pinch today." I graciously smiled.

"Nathan Wolfe?" I heard a familiar voice from behind. Shit.

"Avril. How are you?" I asked as I turned around.

"I'm good. Reverted to school aged children now?" Her brow arched.

"Very funny. I'm picking up the daughter of a friend. She had to work, and her babysitter is sick."

"Wow. This is a new one for you."

"May I ask what you're doing here? You don't have kids."

"Picking up my brother's kid. I babysit him now a couple days a week since his mom passed away."

"Sorry to hear that."

"I'm still waiting for that third date you promised me a few months back."

"Yeah. Sorry about that. My work schedule has been all over the place. Things have been crazy."

The bell rang and a mob of children came running out the doors.

"Nathan!" Ruby exclaimed as she came running up to me.

"It was nice to see you again, Avril. Have a good day." I grabbed Ruby by the hand and led her down the street as fast as I could.

"Why are we walking so fast? Who was that lady?"

"Just an old friend of mine. I haven't seen her in a while."

"Was she your girlfriend?"

"God no. I mean, no, she's just a friend. How would you like to go get some ice cream before we head home?"

"Really?" Her face beamed with excitement.

We stepped into the ice cream parlor and stood in front of the cases staring at the different kinds of ice cream.

"What would you like?" I asked.

"Chocolate chip cookie dough in a waffle cone, please," she said.

"Really?" I cocked my head at her. "That's my favorite too."

"That's because we're cool." She grinned as she high fived me.

I ordered our cones and we took a seat at a table against the window. I heard my phone ding and when I pulled it from my pocket, there was a text message from Allison.

"Just making sure you found Ruby okay."

"I did and she's fine. We're sitting in an ice parlor having ice cream before we head home."

"Thank you, Nathan. I have to get back inside the courtroom. I'll see you later."

"Was that my mom?" Ruby asked.

"Yeah. How did you know?"

"I figured. She worries a lot."

"I feel ya, kid. My mom worries a lot too." I sighed.

As we were enjoying our ice cream, there was a light knock on the window next to us. When I looked over, I saw Mason standing there pointing at me. I rolled my eyes at him and hoped he'd go away, but he didn't. He decided to come in and harass me.

"So, what's going on here? Hey, Ruby." He smiled at her.

"Hi, Mason. Nathan's babysitting me while my mom is at work. After we finish our ice cream, we're going back to his place and he's going to teach me more chords on the guitar."

"Wow. That's nice of you, bro."

"Yeah. Yeah. I thought you were going back to work today."

"I go back tomorrow."

"Want some ice cream?" Ruby asked him.

"Nah. I'm good. But thanks anyway. I have to go. I was just on my way to the store when I spotted the two of you through the window."

The corners of his mouth curved upward. "I'll be calling you later, Nathan."

"I'm sure you will be." I narrowed my eye at him.

"Bye, Ruby. Enjoy your ice cream and your time with Nathan."

"I will." She giggled.

CHAPTER 36

Nathan

We stepped inside my apartment and Ruby threw her backpack on the floor. Picking it up, I asked her if she had any homework to do.

"Nope. I finished it in school. Can I play your guitar now?"

"Sure." I smiled as I grabbed it from the corner and handed it to her.

"Nathan," she spoke in a soft voice.

"Yes, Ruby."

"I'm really sorry about how I acted when we first met." She looked down. It's just—"

"Just what, love?" I asked as I placed my hand on her shoulder.

"There was something about you that reminded me of my dad. I miss him," she said as she looked down.

Shit.

"I know you do, and I'm sorry for your loss."

"My mom cries every night."

"She does?"

"Yeah. She doesn't think I can hear her, but I do. She goes in the bathroom and turns on the shower first. I thought maybe after we moved back here, she wouldn't anymore, but she still does."

I needed to change the subject fast because I was getting very uncomfortable and I didn't know what to say to her.

"Your mom is a strong woman, Ruby. Hey, she'll be getting off work soon. How about we surprise her with some Chinese for dinner, so she doesn't have to cook. You like Chinese food, right?"

"Yeah. I love it." She grinned.

"Great. I'll go get the menu and we'll look it over."

*

Allison

I grabbed my purse and my briefcase and dropped it off at my apartment before going to pick up Ruby. I was so thankful that Nathan offered to watch her for me, but it also felt a little weird. Knocking on the door, Ruby opened it with a smile on her face.

"Hey, Mom." She hugged me.

"Hey, sweetheart."

"You're just in time." Nathan smiled. "I ordered us some Chinese food for dinner. Ruby told me what you like."

"Wow. Thank you. I was going to make hot dogs and macaroni and cheese."

"Sorry, Mom. Chinese food is way better," Ruby said.

"How was court?" he asked as took the cartons of food out of the bag.

"It was good. We won."

"Excellent." He grinned.

"You guys are playing Monopoly?" I asked as I saw it set up on the floor.

"Yeah and I'm kicking Nathan's butt!"

"Your daughter is a cheater. Just like Elijah. I'd love to see those two play together."

"It's called strategy, Nathan."

"See. She sounds just like him too." He smirked and I couldn't help but laugh.

As I sat at the table eating with the two of them, suddenly, out of nowhere, I felt as if the air around me was closing in. My heart started to rapidly beat, and I broke out into a sweat.

"Excuse me for a moment. I need to use the bathroom."

I got up, walked to the bathroom and shut the door. Planting my hands on the edge of the sink, I gripped it as I closed my eyes and took in a few deep breaths. Once I calmed myself down, I went back to the table and took my seat.

"Everything okay?" Nathan asked.

"Yeah. Everything is fine. I just drank way too much coffee today." I smiled.

After we ate, Nathan and Ruby went to finish their game and I stayed back to clean up.

"Allison, don't worry about that. I'll clean it up later."

"No. I'm cleaning up. Just finish getting bankrupt by a nine-year-old." I smirked.

"I think I'd rather clean up." He frowned.

"I won!" Ruby shouted as she stood up and did a little dance.

"Make no mistake, kid. The next time we play, I'm winning." He pointed at her.

"Then you better get working on your strategy."

I couldn't help but laugh as I grabbed her backpack.

"We need to go, sweetheart. You need a bath before bed."

"Bye, Nathan." She hugged him as he sat on the floor. "Thanks for today. I had fun."

"You're welcome, kid. Have a good night."

"Ruby, go push the button to the elevator. I'll be out there in a minute."

"Okay, Mom."

Nathan stood up and walked over to me.

"Thank you for everything. Karen is feeling better and will pick Ruby up tomorrow."

"Sure. No problem." He brushed the back of his hand down my cheek.

"I better go," I spoke in a nervous tone.

"Have a good night, Allison."

"You too, Nathan."

As soon as we got back to the apartment, I started the bath for Ruby and went into the bedroom and changed into my pajamas. After pouring a glass of wine, I went in to check on her.

"I think you put way too many bubbles in that water." I smiled.

"You can never have too many bubbles. Hey, Mom?"

"Yeah, sweetheart."

"I really like Nathan and I'm glad he's our friend."

"Me too, Ruby."

"I wouldn't mind if the two of you started dating."

I was in the middle of sipping my wine when she said that and nearly choked to death.

"That's sweet of you, but Nathan and I are just friends."

"Are you scared to start dating again, Mom?"

"What? Where is this coming from?" I asked as I cocked my head at her. "This is not a conversation we should be having, little miss."

"Why? You always tell me that we can talk about anything."

"True. But this is one subject I really don't want to talk about. Finish up your bath. I'm going to go pack your lunch for tomorrow." I tapped her on the nose.

CHAPTER 37

ONE MONTH LATER

*N*athan

When I wasn't working, I was hanging out with Ruby, having sex with Allison whenever we could sneak it in and just overall enjoying life. My mother had asked me to join her for dinner. Elijah and Aspen had plans and Mason was working at the station, so it was just the two of us.

I stepped inside Gramercy Tavern and the hostess led me to the booth where my mother was waiting for me.

"Hello, darling." She smiled as I kissed her cheek before sitting down.

"Hi, Mom."

"I took the liberty of ordering you a scotch." She gestured to the glass sitting in front of me.

"Thank you." The corners of my mouth curved upward as I picked up the glass.

"What have you been up to? We haven't really had a chance to sit down and talk alone since your brother's wedding, she spoke as she opened the menu and looked it over.

"Not much. How about you?"

"I've been quite busy at the firm. I spoke to Allison today. Have you spoken to her since the wedding?"

"Here and there." I sipped my drink.

"Are the two of you still having sex?"

"That's really none of your business, Mother."

"I'll take that as a yes. Ruby's babysitter dropped her off at the firm yesterday after school. Apparently, she had some appointment she needed to get to. Allison asked me if it was okay and of course I told her yes. Ruby is an adorable little girl. Don't you think?"

"Yeah. She's a cute kid."

"She told me how much fun she had when you picked her up from school one day. She told me how you took her for ice cream and how she beat you in Monopoly."

"Okay? What's your point?" I asked with an arch in my brow.

"Is there something going on between you and Allison? Besides sex."

"No. Of course not. Allison was in a pinch for a babysitter since her parents were out of town and her babysitter was sick, so I volunteered to help out. I wasn't doing anything anyway."

"That was very nice of you, darling, but it isn't you. Nobody knows you like I do. So spill it. What's going on?"

The waiter walked over as soon as I closed my menu and took our dinner order.

"Another scotch, please. Nothing is going on. We're friends and that's it."

"Friends who have sex." Her brow arched as she picked up her glass of wine.

"Like you can talk, Mother."

"I adore Allison and I don't want to see her get hurt."

"Allison knows exactly where I stand when it comes to relationships and she knows how I am. We had a full conversation about it. It's just casual sex between us."

"Then obviously she took my advice." A smirk crossed her lips.

"Advice? What advice?" I asked as I narrowed my eye at her.

"We had a little chat in Vegas. She told me she hadn't been the same since her husband passed away and would feel guilty for being with another man. I simply told her that there was nothing wrong with having a little casual sex to get her through the day. You're welcome." She smiled. "But if you don't intend on taking it any further with her, you need to cut it off now before it's too late and someone gets hurt."

I sighed as I cut into my steak.

The next morning, I got up early, threw on my running clothes and stepped inside the elevator. As it was going down, it stopped on the twenty-second floor. The doors opened and I saw Allison and Ruby standing there.

"Nathan!" Ruby exclaimed.

"Good morning, sunshine." I smiled as I patted her head. "Good morning, Allison."

"Good morning." A bright smile graced her face as they both stepped inside.

"Off to school?" I asked Ruby.

"Yeah. My Uncle Rick is picking me up today and I'm spending the night at his house. Him and Aunt Darcy are taking me to the movies."

"Sounds like you're going to have some serious fun."

"Do you have any plans for tonight?" she asked as the elevator continued down to the lobby.

"I'm not sure yet."

"My mom doesn't. Maybe you can come down and keep her company while I'm gone."

"Ruby!" Allison said.

The doors opened and I held it with my hand while Allison and Ruby stepped out first.

"Bye Nathan." Ruby waved.

"Bye, Ruby. Have a good day at school. I'll call you later." I mouthed to Allison and she gave me a smile.

While I ran in Central Park, I'd given a lot of thought to the conversation my mother and I had last night. As delusional as I was to think that me and Allison could keep having sex without any consequences, I knew it would only be a matter of time. A matter of time before I hurt her. Not to mention a matter of time before Elijah found out and kicked my ass. It was only supposed to be a one-time thing. Then it turned into multiple times and dinners with the three of us, guitar lessons, monopoly games, video games and dancing and singing to The Beatles in the middle of the living room. My entire world had been turned upside down since I'd met them and when I saw my future, I saw the three of us in it, but I also saw the heartache and misery that followed. I saw the fear in my heart and in my soul, and the destruction I'd leave behind. The fear of "normal" suffocated me and I knew what had to be done.

I stopped running and tried to regain my breath. Pulling out my phone, I saw I had a text message from Allison.

"Dinner tonight? My place?"

"Sounds good. I'll see you around seven."

"Can't wait. Heading into court now. TTYL."

I took in a deep breath as tonight would be the night. The night I had to have a talk with Allison. A talk I dreaded.

CHAPTER 38

Allison

I couldn't wait any longer for Nathan to call me, so I sent him a text message inviting him over for dinner. The past month had been a whirlwind of emotions. I never thought I'd fall for someone again after Jared, but I did. The more time Nathan and I spent together, the more I fell for him. And watching him with Ruby was the icing on the cake. She loved him and she was happier when he was around. I knew she missed her father terribly, but if she could find it in her heart to let someone else inside, I could too. I knew how Nathan felt about relationships, but maybe I was different to him. I prayed I was because when I saw my future now, I saw him in it. I was ready. As much as it scared me, I was willing to try. He made me happy and he made me laugh. He made me forget about the loneliness that hid inside me. We had so much in common that it was kind of scary. We liked all the same things and we had this habit of finishing each other's sentences. We fit together and I didn't want to hide anymore. I wanted to introduce him to my father and to Rick and Darcy, and I wanted Elijah to know. Tonight would be the night that I would tell him how I felt, and I prayed he felt the same way.

"What's that smile for?" Elijah asked as he stepped into my office.

"No reason. Just happy in life."

"Excellent. That's what I like to hear. It doesn't happen to be because of a man, does it? Because I know that look you women get."

"Is that so?" I smiled. "Actually, it does have to do with someone that I met. He's coming over tonight for dinner."

"I hope he's a nice guy because if he's not, he'll have me to deal with." He smirked.

"He is a nice guy. In fact, he's a great guy. I never thought I'd ever meet someone again after Jared, but I did and honestly, I really like him."

"I'm happy to hear that, Allison. You deserve to be happy. When can I meet him? Maybe the four of us can have dinner next week."

"Sounds good. I'm sure he'll like that."

"Just let me know. Here's the file for the Clarence case. Do me a favor and look it over and see if I missed anything."

"Will do, Elijah."

He walked to the door, stopped and turned around.

"Have fun tonight, Allison, and have a good weekend."

"I will, Elijah. You too. I'll see you on Monday."

※

I got held up at the office and didn't get home until fifteen minutes before Nathan was to arrive. So, I stopped at the Indian place around the corner and picked us up some food. When I got home, I quickly changed into something more comfortable, touched up my makeup and ran a brush through my hair.

It was seven o'clock on the dot when there was a knock at my door. Opening it, a smile crossed my lips when I saw Nathan standing there looking as sexy as ever.

"Hey there," I reached up and brushed my lips against his.

"Hey yourself." His hands gripped my hips.

"Come in. I stopped on the way home and picked up some food from that Indian place around the corner. I got held up at the office."

"You should have let me know. I would have picked it up."

"It was on the way home. No big deal."

I pulled down two plates as Nathan went into the drawer and grabbed the silverware.

"Beer or wine?" I asked opening the refrigerator.

"Beer sounds good."

I grabbed two bottles and took them over to the table where we sat down and began to eat. We talked about our day. I wanted to wait until after dinner to have my talk with him. I was nervous as hell and I wasn't sure how I was going to start the conversation.

"Did I tell you what Ruby said to me?" I spoke as I placed the dishes in the dishwasher.

"I don't think so. What did she say?"

"She told me that she wouldn't mind if we dated. Do you believe that?" I turned and looked at him with a smile.

"Really? She said that?"

"For her to say that is a big deal. It seems you have charmed your way into her life."

"What did you tell her?"

"I said we were friends."

"Good. That's good." I noticed a nervousness in his voice.

Something was off with him tonight, and I sensed it the minute he walked through the door. I needed to just come out and tell him how I felt.

"There's something I need to talk to you about, Allison."

"There's something I need to talk to you about as well. Me first." I walked over and took hold of his hand. "A year ago after Jared passed away, I never thought I'd met anyone again. I loved him so much and I didn't think it was possible for me to ever love anyone else. But then I met you and as hard as I tried to resist you, I couldn't. Nathan, you gave life to the part of me that died the day Jared passed away. The part of me I never thought would feel again."

"Allison, stop." He pulled away.

"What? What's wrong?"

CHAPTER 39

Nathan

I couldn't believe this. I came here tonight to tell her that we couldn't see each other anymore and there she stood practically telling me that she loved me.

"I can't do this anymore. That's what I wanted to talk to you about. God, this shouldn't be this hard." I rubbed the back of my neck as I paced around the room.

"Can't do what, Nathan?"

I turned around and stared into her teary eyes which made it a thousand times worse.

"I like you, Allison. I really do. But we can't keep doing this. Things are spinning out of control and this is the only way I know how to stop it. The last thing I want to do is hurt you. You don't deserve it. I think it's in both our best interest that we stop seeing each other."

"If this is because of what I just told—"

"It has nothing to do with that. My mind was already made up before I walked through the door."

She stared at me as a tear rolled down her cheek.

"Why? Why are you doing this?" she shouted.

"You want the damn truth, Allison?" I raised my voice at her. "Because I'm mad at you. I'm fucking mad."

"Why? What did I do to make you so angry?" Another tear fell from her eyes.

"You made me care. That's what you did. You made me care about you and you made me care about your little girl. I told you that I don't do relationships. No matter how good things are or how in love you are, the other person could always just lose feelings for you and be gone just like that." I snapped my fingers. "And something like that isn't in any of our control. I made a mistake and I shouldn't have let it go on."

"Get out," she spoke in a calm tone.

"Allison, please—"

"God, I feel like such an idiot. I should have known better in the first place. What did I expect? This is what you do, and this is who you are. Men like you don't change. You're not a man, Nathan Wolfe, you're a coward and a user. You had your fun with me and now it's time to move on and seek out the next thrill."

"Allison." I slowly shook my head. "That is not true."

"Don't you dare lie to me," she shouted as she pointed her finger. "Get out of my fucking apartment right now!"

"I'm so sorry. I truly am."

"GET OUT!" she screamed as the tears flowed down her face.

I walked out of her apartment and headed to the elevator. My heart was racing, and a sickness formed in the pit of my stomach. The minute I stepped into my apartment, I picked up the bottle of scotch and started drinking it until I passed out.

❧

*A*llison
I threw myself on the bed and cried as I curled into a ball. My heart was shattered, and the pain was too much to deal with. Was this my punishment for trying to move on?

"Haven't I suffered enough?" I shouted as I stared up at the ceiling.

"Wasn't it enough for you to take my husband away from me? What the fuck did I ever do that was so wrong to deserve this in my life?"

I forced myself to get up and change into my pajamas. Climbing back into bed, I stayed there and cried until I fell asleep.

The next morning as I struggled to open my swollen eyes, I picked up my phone and looked at the time. It was ten o'clock and there was a text message from my brother Rick.

"Hey, sis. We'll be dropping Ruby off around five o'clock."

"Thanks, Rick. I'll be here."

Ruby. How was I going to tell her that she won't be seeing Nathan around anymore? She was going to be devastated and once again, her little heart would be broken. What the hell was I going to say? Humiliation soared through me. I should have let him talk first. Not that it wouldn't have made a difference. The only difference would've been that I wouldn't have given him the satisfaction of telling him how I felt. Oh my God, I was such an idiot. I took in a deep breath, got myself out of bed and took a shower for I needed to go grocery shopping before Ruby got home. As much as I didn't want to leave my apartment, I had no choice.

CHAPTER 40

Nathan

I awoke to someone knocking on my door. Picking up my phone to check the time, I had several text messages from Mason.

"Bro, I thought we were meeting at the gym. I'm here and you're not."

"Seriously? The least you could have done was tell me you weren't coming."

"Bro, it's been two hours and I haven't heard from you. Douchebag."

"It's two p.m. This isn't like you. I'm coming over and you better answer the damn door."

I sighed as I struggled to get out of bed. Walking to the door, I opened it, turned away and headed to the kitchen.

"Jesus Christ," Mason said. "Are you hungover or something?"

He stepped inside and picked up the empty bottle of scotch off the floor.

"Nathan, what is going on?"

I reached in the cabinet and picked up the bottle of aspirin.

"I fucked up. That's what's going on."

"What the hell happened last night? Go sit down. I'll make you some coffee."

"I went to Allison's last night to tell her that I didn't want to see her anymore, but before I could, she pretty much told me that she's in love with me and wanted to take things further."

"Shit. I knew this was going to happen. So after she professed her love to you, you told her it was over?"

"Yeah." I placed my hand on my aching head.

"How did she take it?" He set the coffee mug down in front of me.

"How the hell do you think she took it? She was crying, angry, upset. It killed me to see her like that. She told me that I was nothing but a coward and a user and now that I'd had my fun with her it was time to seek out the next thrill. Then she threw me out of her apartment."

"Damn." He slowly shook his head. "Did you do the right thing? Honestly, Nathan, did you?"

"Yeah. I did. Things were getting out of control. I was spending a lot of my time with her and Ruby, and I was only making it worse."

"Worse for who? You or them?"

"Them, of course." I looked up at him.

"Are you sure about that? Listen, bro, I love you, but I think you're an idiot. I've seen you with Allison and it wasn't just a casual fling. No matter how much you tried to convince yourself it was, it wasn't. The way you looked at her was completely different than the way you look at other women. You invested your time with her and Ruby, and you don't do shit like that. No one has ever made you do that. Hell, you're probably even in love with her and that's why you're so freaked out."

"It doesn't matter. What's done is done. She'll get over it. She's a strong woman."

"She just got over her husband's death and now she has to deal with this?"

"What the hell do you want me to do?" I slammed my fist on the table as I got up from my chair.

"I want you to be real with yourself," he shouted. "Own the truth, bro. Just fucking own the truth. You broke it off because you're scared. You're scared of loving someone other than your family. Because in the end, you're scared you're going to be just like Dad."

"His blood runs through us, Mason."

"Yeah. I know that, and I wish to God it didn't. But how long are we going to let him and his actions control our lives? Elijah didn't."

"Elijah's weak."

"No, bro. You're the weak one. We both are," he softly voiced as he lowered his head. "I have to go. I need to run by the station." He got up from his chair. "You better pray to God Elijah doesn't find out about this because I don't know if I can save you this time."

Allison

Ruby had been asking about Nathan all weekend. She wanted to see him, and I had to lie and tell her he was busy. Every time we left the apartment, I was paranoid that we were going to run into each other. Because if we did, Ruby would know something was going on. How long was I going to be able to keep this from her? She was a smart kid and she'd figure it out sooner or later. Damn it. This wasn't just about me. How could I have been so selfish? My job as a mother was to protect my daughter, and I failed because I let my guard down.

It was Monday morning and after dropping Ruby off at school, I headed to the office. The knot in my stomach was as tight as it could get and the ache in my heart hurt like a bitch. I had a hard time controlling the tears but managed to stop them from flowing when Ruby was around. I didn't need her seeing me like that.

"Morning, Bailey," I spoke as I headed into my office.

"Good morning, Allison. Elijah asked to see you in his office."

"Okay. I'll go down in a second."

Great. Did Nathan tell Elijah everything? Is that why he wanted to see me? How the hell was I going to face him without breaking down? I took in a deep breath and headed to his office.

"You wanted to see me, Elijah?"

"Allison, Good morning. Come on in and shut the door. Have a seat." He gestured. "I have a new case for you. But first, how was your date on Friday night?" he asked with a smile.

That was it. That question was all it took for me to turn into a blubbering idiot in front of my boss.

"It didn't go so well," I softly spoke as I lowered my head and a few tears started to fall.

"Oh God, Allison." He got up from his seat and walked over to me. "I'm sorry." He pulled a tissue from the box on his desk and handed it to me.

"Thanks. But don't be. I was the one who was stupid and let my guard down when I knew better."

"You're not stupid, Allison. You met someone you thought could potentially fill the void in your life. There's nothing wrong with that. Sometimes things work out and sometimes they don't. I know you don't want to hear this right now, but there are plenty of guys out there that would kill to date you. You're a beautiful woman and you're smart. Don't let one douchebag who can't see what's in front of him hurt you. It's his loss and someone else's gain."

If only he knew that douchebag was his own brother.

"Thanks, Elijah. But there won't be anybody else for a very long time. I've learned my lesson."

"Allison. Don't let one rotten apple spoil it for the rest of the good apples."

I looked up at him and couldn't help but let out a light laugh.

"I know. It's cheesy, right? But it's true. The good guys outweigh the douchebag ones. Don't forget this Saturday night is the fundraising gala the firm puts on every year. If you need a babysitter for Ruby, our nanny would be more than happy to watch her while she's with Mila."

"Thanks. Ruby is going to be with Jared's parents this weekend. They're taking her to Long Island so she can play with her cousins."

"Okay. Just thought I'd throw the offer out there."

"Thanks for the pep talk." I got up from my chair and took the file folder on his desk. "

"Do you need to take the day off? I'll understand if you need to."

"No. I'm okay. I just need to keep busy." I gave him a small smile.

CHAPTER 41

*A*llison

On the way home from work, I stopped and picked up a pizza for dinner. I'd decided that I needed to tell Ruby that Nathan wouldn't be coming around anymore. I couldn't keep it from her any longer and the more time that went by, the worse it would be. I needed to be honest with her, to an extent.

"Yay. You brought home pizza!" Ruby exclaimed as she ran to me the moment I stepped through the door.

"I got your favorite." I smiled as I set the box on the island.

After saying goodbye to my Mom, I grabbed two paper plates and set them on the table.

"How was your day?" I asked her.

"It was okay. We're having career day next week and I'm going to ask Nathan if he'd come and speak to my class about being a pilot." She beamed with excitement.

I took in a deep breath before crushing my little girl and her heart.

"Listen, Ruby. I don't know if Nathan will be able to do that."

"Why?"

I swallowed the lump that was stuck in my throat.

"Nathan won't be coming around anymore. We decided we shouldn't be friends anymore."

"Why?" She looked down in disappointment. "Did you get into a fight?"

"A small one."

"About what?"

"Just grown up stuff." I could feel the sting in my eyes.

"Can't you just make up? Friends get in fights all the time. You and Daddy fought sometimes, and you made up."

"That was different. Daddy and I were married."

"What was the fight about? I want to know," she shouted. "You told me that you would never keep things from me. You promised. You were happy when he was around. You stopped crying over Dad. What happened?" She stood up from her chair. "Just because you aren't friends anymore doesn't mean that I can't be friends with him!" she yelled across the table and I lost it.

"He doesn't want to see us anymore, Ruby! He's the one who came here and told me. He said things were getting out of control and he needed to put an end to it." No matter how hard I tried to hold it together, I couldn't do it anymore.

Ruby walked over to me and placed her hands on each side of my face.

"Why would he do that?" she asked in soft voice.

"I don't know, sweetheart. He obviously has some personal issues, and if that's the case, then we're better off without him in our lives." A tear rolled down my cheek.

"He hurt you." She wrapped her arms around my neck.

"He hurt my heart. That's all."

"I'm sorry, Mom. I love you and I'm here for you."

"I love you too, sweetie, and I know you are. You've been so strong through everything and I'm so proud of you." I hugged her tight.

"It'll be okay, Mom."

"Thanks, sweetie. Listen, I have to attend a gala for the firm on Friday night and I need a new dress. How about we play hooky tomorrow from work and school, sleep in and go shopping and out to lunch?"

"Really?" She grinned.

"Yeah. Really." I tapped her on the nose.

"Elijah won't mind?"

"No. I'll text him and let him know."

"Is it okay if I sleep with you tonight?" she asked.

"Of course it is. I'd love the company. In fact, let's go get in our pajamas, climb in bed and watch a movie."

"Okay!"

Two Weeks Later

Nathan

The past couple of weeks at work had me flying short trips. Short enough that it allowed me to come home every night, which I hated. This was definitely a time where I longed for flights that kept me out of New York. On Saturday, I had my mother's gala I had to attend. I didn't feel like going because I knew Allison would be there and I hadn't seen or talked to her since that night. I knew it was a long shot, but I picked up my phone and called my mother.

"Hello, darling."

"Hey, Mom. Listen, about the gala tonight. I'm not sure I'm going to be able to attend."

"Unless you're dying and are in the hospital, it's not an option. Are you dying or in the hospital?"

I rolled my eyes.

"No."

"Then I'll see you tonight at six-thirty sharp. You know how important this is to me every year."

"I know. I'll see you tonight." I sighed as I ended the call.

Allison had been on my mind the past couple of weeks and no matter what I did, I couldn't stop thinking about her. I missed her and

I missed Ruby. The worse part was I couldn't even drink like I wanted to because I had to be up early every morning for work.

I needed to stop by Elijah's house to pick up some cufflinks he was lending me since I'd seemed to have lost my pair one night in a hotel room with some random chick.

I took the private elevator up to the penthouse and when the doors opened, Aspen came walking into the foyer.

"Hey, sis." I kissed her cheek. "Where's my niece?"

"She's in the kitchen. Elijah is feeding her breakfast. Can I get you a cup of coffee?"

"That would be great. Hey, bro," I said as I walked into the kitchen.

"Hey. I haven't heard from you in a while. I was starting to get worried."

"It's been a busy past couple of weeks with work. Hey, sweet girl." I smiled at Mila in her highchair as I kissed her head.

She held her arms up to me.

"I think she wants you to feed her." A smirk crossed Elijah's lips as he handed me the baby food jar and spoon.

Aspen set the coffee cup down in front of me as I started feeding the baby.

"This shi—stuff smells pretty good." I looked at the jar and saw it was bananas.

"So far it's her favorite. I dare you to take a taste." My brother grinned.

"No, thanks, bro. I'm good. How's work going?" I asked.

"Busy. Very busy. We're getting bombarded with new cases every day. I just hope I'm not overwhelming Allison. By the way, have you seen her?" he asked.

"No. I haven't seen her at all. Why?" I asked with suspicion.

"Just wondering if you happened to see who the guy is she was seeing. Things didn't work out."

"No. I didn't know she was seeing anyone," I carefully spoke as I brought the spoon up to Mila's mouth.

"You haven't seen any strange guys hanging around the building?"

"Nope. I haven't noticed. Is she okay?"

"Nah, she's really broken up over the whole thing. She started crying in my office."

Did he know and he was just beating around the bush about it?

"Man, that sucks. Did you offer her some advice?"

"I told her that she was a beautiful and smart woman and not to let one rotten apple spoil it for the good apples. I told her that there are plenty of guys out there who would kill to date her. And don't go getting any ideas." He pointed at me.

Whew. He didn't know.

"You don't have to worry about that," I said as Mila spit out a mouth of food at me.

Elijah laughed and wiped her mouth with a soft washcloth.

"I'll go get those cufflinks. I'll be right back."

Aspen walked back into the kitchen, cleaned Mila up and took her from her highchair.

"I know you're the one who broke Allison's heart," she whispered to me.

"I don't know what you're talking about," I nervously spoke.

"You damn Wolfe boys." She shook her head. "I'm not stupid, Nathan. We women have a sense for this kind of stuff."

"I can't talk about this right now. Elijah will be coming back."

"I hid the cufflinks, so he'll be a while." She smiled. "She's a wonderful woman. You had happiness staring you straight in the face and you turned your back on it."

"It's complicated, Aspen."

"Of course it is. Everything with you Wolfe boys is complicated."

"Here you go," Elijah set the cufflinks down in front of me.

"Thanks, bro. I should get going. I have things to do before tonight."

"Are you and Allison coming together?" Elijah asked.

"Why would we?"

"Because you live in the same building and you're both going to the same place. Maybe you should ask her. I'm sure she could use the company right now."

Shit. Shit. Shit.

"You know, as much as I'd love to, I can't. I'm actually seeing someone before I head over to the hotel."

"Oh. Okay." He patted my back. "I'll see you later then."

Was that a test?

Mila held her arms out to me, trying to get out of Aspen's grip. I took her in my arms, kissed her head and held for a moment before I left.

CHAPTER 42

Allison

I had walked into my apartment building from having my hair done when I saw Nathan standing at the elevator. Quickly, I turned around and walked out and down a half a block until I knew it was safe. It was bad enough I'd have to see him tonight, but at least it would be in a room full of people. There was no way I was about to get in an elevator alone with him.

I changed into my red, floor length strapless gown with the thigh-high slit and sweetheart neckline. This event was black tie and formal attire was required. I knew a lot of the women were going to be dressed in black, so I opted to be bold and go for red. I felt glamourous in my dress and my elegant up do. I rummaged through my jewelry and pulled out a simple, but elegant diamond necklace Jared had given me for our anniversary with the diamond bracelet to match. Slipping into my red strappy heels, I grabbed my clutch and headed out the door.

I pushed the button to the elevator and when it stopped on my floor, the doors opened, and Nathan and two other people stood there staring at me. I swallowed hard as my heart raced and I stepped inside, avoiding his stare.

"You look simply gorgeous, my dear," An older woman spoke. "Fancy party tonight?"

"Thank you." I nervously smiled at her. "And yes, I'm going to a fancy party."

"You're going to have trouble with the men tonight, young lady." Her husband grinned at me.

I gave him a small smile as the doors opened and I quickly stepped out.

"Allison," I heard Nathan's voice from behind. I ignored him and walked out of the building. "Will you stop for a minute, please."

"Leave me alone, Nathan, "I said as I held up my hand for a cab.

"Listen, since we're going to the same place, let's just share a cab."

One pulled up and he opened the door for me. I quickly climbed in, grabbed the door handle and looked at him.

"No. Get your own cab." I pulled the door shut. "Can you step on it, please." I spoke to the cab driver.

"Do you know that guy?" The cab driver asked.

"Unfortunately," I replied.

※

Nathan

I sighed as I signaled for another cab. This was going to be a fun night. Damn it. She looked way too sexy and gorgeous. The moment the elevator doors opened, and I saw her standing there, not only did my heart begin to race, but my cock also started to rise.

When I stepped into the ballroom where the event was being held, I quickly grabbed a glass of champagne as the waiter walked by with them on a tray.

"Hello, darling," my mother spoke as she kissed my cheek.

"Hello, Mother. You looked stunning as always."

"Thank you, darling. Your brothers are sitting at our table if you want to head over there."

"Thanks."

I took my champagne and headed over to the table only to find

Allison sitting there next to Elijah and the only empty seat left was next to her. Shit. Like I said, this was going to be a fun evening. I didn't even understand why she was sitting at the family table.

"Hey, everyone," I spoke as I approached the table and took my seat next to Allison. I needed to play it cool or Elijah would get suspicious. I only hoped she would play along. "Allison, you look amazing."

"Thanks," she spoke in a flat tone as she picked up her champagne glass.

"If you'll excuse me, I'm heading up to the bar. Can I get anything for anyone?" I asked.

"I'll go with you," Mason spoke as he got up from his chair.

"Why the fuck am I sitting next to Allison?" I asked Mason as we headed to the bar.

"Bro, I tried to switch the place cards, but Mom caught me and stopped me. I couldn't come up with an excuse fast enough."

"Do you know how awkward this is? I ran into her in the elevator and told her since we were both coming here, we should share a cab. She told me to get my own cab and slammed the door in my face."

He let out a light laugh, and I smacked his shoulder.

"Do you blame her? Come on, Nathan."

"No. I don't blame her, but still. Now I have to sit next to her?"

"Only for dinner. Just eat quick and get up and mingle. Look around. There are some really hot single girls here for you to hit up."

"Under any other circumstances, that would make me happy. But there's only one girl here that interests me."

"And you fucked that right up, bro. You made your bed and now you have lie in it."

"You're a douchebag." I narrowed my eye at him.

"What's going on over here?" Elijah asked as he walked up to us.

"Just some single brotherly talk about the hot chicks here and which ones we're thinking about hitting on." Mason grinned. "Too bad you can't join in the fun."

"You're such a douchebag." He sighed. "Dinner is being served so get back to the table."

As soon as he walked away, I looked at Mason.

"Thanks, bro."

"I always got your back. Let's go eat."

CHAPTER 43

*A*llison
  I'd never been more uncomfortable in my life. Seeing him for the first time since that night intensified the ache in my heart. I wasn't sure if I could do this. Keep up this façade as if nothing was wrong.

"Before we eat, I need to use the ladies' room. Allison, do you need to go?" Aspen asked.

"Actually, I do."

I got up from my seat and followed her into the bathroom. She looked under each stall to make sure no one was in there.

"Are you okay?" she asked.

"I'm fine. Why?"

"Because I know Nathan is the one who broke your heart and now you have to sit next to him."

I looked down as I took in a deep breath and placed my hands on the sink.

"How did you know?"

"I just did. I tried to switch the place cards, but Caitlin saw me and asked what I was doing. She's a real stickler about those damn place cards. Listen." She placed her hand on my arm. "I know what you're going through. These Wolfe boys are a lot to deal with. Trust me. I don't have time to explain right now, but how about we meet for brunch tomorrow? Say around noon?"

"Sure. That'll be great. Jared's parents aren't dropping off Ruby until the evening."

"Okay." She smiled. "We better get out there before the guys get suspicious."

We walked back to the table and I took my seat without even looking at Nathan. I couldn't stand how my aching heart wouldn't calm itself down. I was quiet during dinner and Elijah could sense something was up.

"Are you okay?" he asked.

"Yeah. I'm great." I gave him a smile. "This is really nice. I'm happy I could be a part of it."

"We're all happy to have you here and a part of our firm."

The evening went on and as soon as Nathan finished eating, he got up and walked away, which was fine with me. The moment he left the table I felt as if I could breath again. After Caitlin and Elijah made their speeches, the only two people left at the table were me and Aspen. We started talking about Nathan and made sure nobody was within an earshot of us.

"He went on to say something about no matter how good things are or how in love you are, the other person could always just lose feelings for you and be gone just like that. And something like that isn't in any of our control, and he shouldn't have let it go on."

"What?" Elijah spoke as he stood behind me. "The guy you were seeing said that to you?" He looked over to where Nathan was standing.

"Oh shit. Elijah, no!" Aspen grabbed hold of his arm and he jerked it out from her grip.

Nathan

I was standing talking to Mason when Elijah came up to me, grabbed my arm and dragged me outside.

"What the fuck, bro?" I got out from his grip.

"What the fuck? I'll tell you what the fuck," he said as he punched me square in the face and sent me to the ground. *Shit. He knew about Allison.* Getting up, I tackled him, and we began to fight.

"I fucking warned you to stay away from her," he said as he punched me again. "You did exactly what I knew you'd do."

"It's none of your fucking business, bro. Get over yourself." I threw one last punch before Mason grabbed me and Tommy grabbed Elijah.

"What the hell is going on here?" My mother shouted. "You're both acting like fucking teenagers.

"Ask your son what he did," he said as he got out of Tommy's grip and straightened his suitcoat.

"Elijah," Aspen ran up.

"Not now, Aspen. Allison, I'm sorry, but he deserved it. Consider it a sympathy gift from me," he spoke as he walked back inside the hotel.

I shook my head at Allison as she stood there and stared at me. She looked upset and Aspen took her back inside the hotel.

"What the hell did you do?" My mother demanded to know.

"You know damn well what I did," I growled as I wiped the blood pouring from my lip. "I took your advice."

"I warned you, bro," Mason said.

"Shut the fuck up."

I walked over to the curb and held my hand up at the approaching cab. When it stopped, I climbed in and went home. Grabbing an ice pack from the freezer, I held it on my face. This was payback from Allison after she promised she wouldn't tell him. A few moments later, there was a knock at the door.

"I don't want any—"

"Visitors. I know. I wouldn't either," Allison spoke.

"I thought you were Mason."

"He found your phone in the grass and was going to bring it to you, but I told him I would since I live in the same building and all."

"Thanks. I didn't even realize it was gone."

"Can I come in for a minute?"

"Now's not a good time."

"I promise it'll only take a minute."

"Suit yourself."

"I want you to know that I never told him. He overheard something I said to Aspen and figured it out."

"And what did you say to Aspen?" I narrowed my eye at her.

"I just told her what you said about no matter how good things are or how in love you are—"

"Of course he figured it out." I interrupted her. "Because that's all we heard from our mother growing up." I walked away holding the ice pack on my face.

"I'm sorry, Nathan. I didn't know."

"You wouldn't have known and there's no reason for you to apologize. He was going to find out eventually. I was prepared for this."

"Doesn't matter. What Elijah did was wrong, and you didn't deserve to be punched like that."

"Yeah, Allison, I did deserve it. Now if you don't mind, I'm just going to head to bed. It's been a long night."

"Of course. Good night, Nathan." She lowered her head and walked out the door.

CHAPTER 44

Nathan

I woke up the next morning, sore as fuck and to the ringing sound of my phone. Grabbing it, I saw my mother was calling. Shit. I was in no mood for this.

"Hello."

"Are you up?"

"I am now thanks to you."

"Good. Get showered and dressed and get your ass over to my house. You have one hour to be here."

"Mom, seriously?"

"I said one hour, Nathan Michael Wolfe!" Click.

As soon as I got dressed, I headed over to her townhouse. As I climbed out of the cab, Elijah's limo pulled up behind me. Jesus Christ.

"I figured she summoned you as well," Elijah spoke as he climbed out of the car.

"I'm not surprised she called you either."

He walked over to me and took a look at my swollen lip and the bruise across my cheek.

"Not bad. I should have decked you harder."

"By the looks of it, I got you pretty good."

"Boys! In here now!" my mother scowled as she stood at the door.

"Here we go," I spoke as I tucked my hands in my pockets.

"Thank you both for coming."

"Like we had a choice," I said.

"Nathan Michael, enough. Now I want the two of you to sit down in the dining room. I made you a nice brunch and we're going to sit down and discuss the events of last night," she spoke as she placed our plates in front of us. "I'll start first. I didn't appreciate the two of you fighting at my event. Elijah, you could have waited until after to beat on your brother." Her brow raised at him. "And anyway, what Nathan does is really none of your concern."

"Yeah, bro," I said.

"Nathan, shut up." My mother shot me a look. "I know you have an issue with your brothers messing around with the employees at the firm. I for one want you to know that I knew about him and Allison."

"What?!" Elijah exclaimed. "You knew."

"Yes, I did, and he didn't tell me. I caught them. Anyway, I told Nathan that if he didn't have any plans on taking things to the next level with Allison, he was to break it off immediately before someone got hurt. Apparently, he did."

"That's just—" Elijah began to speak, and my mother put her finger up.

"You'll have your turn when I'm finished. Until then, neither one of you are allowed to speak. If I recall, Elijah, you did the same thing to Aspen. So you have no right to judge your brother. In fact, I think this has nothing to do with him sleeping with Allison. I think it has to do with some kind of authority you think you have over your brothers."

"That is—"

"What did I say? You will have your turn when I'm finished."

I couldn't help but sit there with a smirk on my face.

"You have been protective of them since your father left all those years ago. I believe you feel like it's your duty to watch over them, and when they defy you or your orders, you take it personally and as an act of rebellion. I hate to burst your bubble, darling, but you have no right to tell your brother who he can and can't sleep with. Now look at the two of you and look at your faces. You both should be ashamed of yourselves. Playing around is one thing, but to act in a manner of intentional violence towards each other is another, and I will not tolerate such behavior as long as I'm alive. Do you both understand me?" The tone of her voice was stern.

"Yes, Mother," we both spoke at the same time.

"Anything else you'd like to say to me?"

"I'm sorry," we both spoke.

"Good. Apologies accepted. Now finish your brunch and hash it out like the adults you are. I'll be upstairs with Tommy. If I hear even an inkling of an issue down here, there will be consequences."

She walked out of the room and I looked at Elijah.

"What consequences?" I asked.

"Who the hell knows but I don't want to find out. I'm sorry I came after you last night and messed up that pretty face of yours." He smirked.

"It's okay, bro. I'm sorry too. I bet Aspen ripped you a new one last night."

He chuckled. "Yeah, she did. I almost had to sleep in the guest room. Why Allison, Nathan?"

"It all started in the airport. I don't know, bro. There was something about her. Then I found out she moved in my building and then you handed my case over to her. But I will tell you this, I was not responsible for starting it. She came to my suite in Vegas and threw herself at me. It was only supposed to be one time, but then it grew into so much more. The more I got to know her and Ruby, the more I wanted to be with them. You have no idea what I'd done."

"Then tell me."

"We sang songs on the guitar. I taught Ruby a few chords and before I knew it, I was having dinner with them a lot. Hell, I even picked Ruby up from school one day when Allison was in a bind for a babysitter and took her for ice cream. Then we went back to my place and she kicked my ass in Monopoly. The evenings when I wasn't working went from me going out and partying it up to going over to

Allison's to sing and dance around the living room. And the problem was, I liked it. I liked it too much and it freaked me the fuck out."

"I can relate to some of that," he said. "You really sang and danced around the living room?"

"Yes. I did."

A smile crossed his lips as he slowly shook his head.

"One day I woke up and Allison was the only thing I could think about. She consumed my mind day in and day out. When I had to work and not see her for a week or a few days, I hated it. I was miserable, man. That's when I realized things had gotten out of control for me. I had to end it for her. She'd already been through so much with the death of her husband that I didn't want to cause her anymore pain. When I got to her apartment that night, she spilled her soul to me. She told me how I gave life to the part of her that died when her husband did and how she thought she'd never be able to meet anyone again after him. And the sex, damn. Every time it got better and better which I didn't think was possible. Before I knew it, I couldn't even imagine having sex with anyone else but her."

"Do you remember what you said to me standing in the middle of my living room after I broke it off with Aspen?"

"Maybe."

"You told me what you saw when you looked at us together. And the one thing you didn't see was me walking out like Dad did. Bro, I realized I'm nothing like him and neither are you."

"You can't be so sure of that."

"Yes, I can be, and I am. Aspen is the best thing that happened to me, and you knew it before I did because I was consumed with fear. Now I'm going to tell you the same thing you told me. I like Allison a lot and if I had to choose a woman for you to fall in love with, I'd choose her. She's good for you and I think she'd keep you in line like Aspen does with me." He smirked. "It's never too late to start over. All you have to do is push those fears down and go for it. If there's anything I learned, it's that fear holds you back from the most beautiful things in life."

"Wow. Where the fuck did you learn that?"

"Shut up. I've grown up as a man and it's time you do the same. Do you truly love her?"

"I think so. Yes, I do." I corrected myself. "But she'll never forgive me for what I said to her."

"She might. It's going to be tough because women love to punish us, but it's worth the hard work." He smiled.

"Thanks, Elijah."

We both stood up from our chairs and had a bro hug.

"Anytime, little brother."

"My sweet boys. Look at you two. I knew you'd talk it out," My mother spoke as she walked into the room. "I love you both very much."

"We love you too, Mom." We all hugged.

CHAPTER 45

*A*llison

I met Aspen for brunch like we planned. We talked a lot about Elijah and Nathan, and she filled me about their family.

"Elijah did the same thing to me. The boys can't help it. It's in their blood." She laughed. "I can laugh about it now because things are perfect for me and Elijah. But then, I was going through the same thing you are. Nathan will come around. That I can guarantee you. He's just going through the same emotions Elijah went through. They have this fear of becoming like their father."

"I'm over it, Aspen. I've come to realize that maybe I was too quick to get involved with someone again. To be honest, I don't think it's in the cards for me anyway."

"Stop that." She placed her hand on mine. "Why do you think that."

I could feel the tears swelling in my eyes.

"Because I lost my husband at such a young age. Then I met Nathan and let my guard down and he left me too. I just need to put all my focus on raising my daughter alone, without the complications of a man in my life."

"Do you love Nathan?"

"I thought I did. But now, I don't know. I think I was just all caught up in the awesome sex. You know how that messes with our heads."

She gave me a small smile as she gently squeezed my hand.

After I left the restaurant, I headed home, and as I approached my building from the left, Nathan was approaching from the right.

"Hey, Allison," he said as held the door open for me.

"Hey. Thanks. Your face." I gave him a sympathetic look.

"Nah. It's not so bad. You should see Elijah." He smiled.

"You saw him?" I asked as we walked to the elevator.

"Yeah. My mother summoned both of us to her house and we couldn't leave until we talked things out."

"Got to love our mothers." I smiled.

"All is good. We had a long talk."

"Good. I'm happy to hear that."

The elevator doors opened and we both stepped inside.

"Where's Ruby?"

"She's with Jared's parents. She spent the weekend over there."

"Nice. I'm sure she's having a good time."

"Yeah." I looked down. "They'll be dropping her off in couple of hours. I actually just came from having brunch with Aspen."

"Oh really? Did she tell you how she ripped Elijah a new one last night?" The corners of his mouth curved upward.

"She did." I laughed.

Suddenly, he reached over and placed his thumb on my chin, and I could feel my body start to tremble.

"It's good to see you smile."

The elevator doors opened, and I stepped out.

"Enjoy the rest of your day," I nervously spoke as my heart raced.

"Allison, wait." He held the door open with his hand.

"Yeah."

"I'm sorry for everything."

"Me too, Nathan. I have to go."

"Wait. Since Ruby isn't home, can we talk?"

"There's nothing to talk about. I said what I said, and you said what you said. We both said enough, and I just want to leave it in the past and move on."

"Move on alone?"

"Yes. Alone. I really have to go."

I stepped inside my apartment and quickly shut the door. Letting out a deep breath, I slid down it until I hit the ground and placed my hand on my forehead. Suddenly, there was a knock on the door that scared the shit out of me.

"Oh my God, will you leave—Caitlin, I'm so sorry. I thought you were someone else."

"Is this a bad time, darling?"

"No. Please, come in." I gestured.

"Where's that adorable little girl of yours?"

"She's with her grandparents. They'll be home in a couple hours. What are you doing here?" I cocked my head.

"Meddling in my son's life like I always do. But seriously, I think we need to have a little chat."

"Okay. Can I make you some coffee?"

"No, thank you." She smiled.

"Listen, Caitlin, if you came to have a little chat about Nathan, I'm not interested."

"Well, it is about him and I'm sorry, but I need you to listen to me. I know you're hurting right now, and I don't blame you. Trust me. I've been there myself more times than I care to remember. My sons have issues. We all do." She rolled her eyes. "I don't think we'd be human if we didn't. But I take full responsibility for all their issues. Growing up with me as a single parent was difficult for them and I tried the best I could. But I also planted in their minds that relationships are no good and nothing lasts forever. I kept reminding them over and over what their father had done and how he left them. I placed that fear inside my boys and I regret it. If I could take it back, I would."

"Caitlin, the boys have their own minds."

"I know, but somewhere in the back of all the chaos going on in their heads, they hear my voice. I'm sorry that Nathan broke your heart, but it wasn't because he doesn't want to be with you. It's because he's scared and he's trying to protect you. I better go. Think about our little chat."

"I will. Thanks for stopping by." A small smile crossed my lips.

"You're welcome, darling. I'll see you tomorrow at the office." She headed towards the door, and when she placed her hand on the handle, she turned to me. "If by some chance you choose to forgive him, make him work for it first." She gave me a wink and walked out the door.

CHAPTER 46

ONE WEEK LATER

Nathan

It was the last day of a four-day shift and believe it or not, it felt good to be home. Tomorrow was Elijah's birthday party and I was lucky enough to have made it back in time. I hadn't seen Allison all week due to my flight schedule. I flew out the day after our last conversation in the elevator. I'd thought about texting her a few times while I was gone, but I was afraid she wouldn't reply. It seemed as though she couldn't get away from me fast enough that day.

As tired as I was, I wanted to go for a run, so I changed into my running clothes, grabbed my phone and my key and stepped onto the elevator. It stopped on the twenty-second floor and when the doors opened, Ruby was standing there.

"Hey there, Miss Ruby." I smiled.

She stepped into the elevator and didn't say a word.

"Are you headed down to the art room?"

Still no words came out of her mouth.

The elevator made it to the tenth floor, jerked, and then came to a complete stop.

"What the hell! Not again," I said.

"Great." Ruby rolled her eyes as she sat down and crossed her legs.

"When I get off this thing, I'm having a long talk with the manager. This is getting ridiculous. Are you okay down there?" I asked.

She stared down at the ground and wouldn't look at me. I sighed as I sat down next to her.

"You're mad at me, aren't you?" I asked.

"Yeah. I'm mad at you."

"Listen, kid. I'm mad at myself too. I messed up in a big way and I'm really sorry."

"You are?" She glanced at me.

"Yeah. I am. More than you'll ever know."

"You hurt my mom's heart." She looked down and I could hear the sadness in her voice.

"I know I did, love, and I regret it. I want to make things right. I like your mom a lot and I miss you both."

"My mom said you have personal issues and we're better off without you in our lives."

"She said that?" I cocked my head.

"Yeah."

"Truth is, I do have some personal issues and I'm working on them. I want you and your mom in my life. I don't want to stay away anymore."

"Then you need to tell her that."

"I tried and she wouldn't listen. Then I had to leave for four days for work and I haven't been able to talk to her since. How is she doing?"

"She's okay. She's not as happy as she was when you were around."

"I'm sorry about that, kid. But I promise you this, I'm going to do everything I can to get her to forgive me? If I need your help, are you in?" I smiled at her as I held out my hand.

"I'm in." She placed her hand in mine. "I'm going to warn you right now, if you hurt her again, you'll have me to deal with." Her eyes narrowed at me and I couldn't help but laugh.

"I promise I'm not going to hurt her or you ever again."

Finally, the elevator started going down and we made it to the lobby. As the doors opened, Ruby took hold of my hand.

"Will you come to the art room and paint a picture with me?" she asked in a sweet innocent voice.

"Sure." I smiled.

※

Allison

"We the jury, find the defendant not guilty."

I let out a deep breath as Elijah glanced over at me with a smile on his face.

"Excellent work, Allison."

"Thank you. I had my doubts for a minute."

"I didn't." He gave me a wink.

We packed up our briefcases, said goodbye to our client and headed out of the courthouse.

"You're coming to the party tomorrow night, right?" Elijah asked as we walked back to the office.

"Yes. Of course. I wouldn't miss it for the world." I smiled.

"Good. Listen, why don't you just go straight home. The case is finished, and you deserve to go home early."

"Are you sure?"

"Positive. Have a great night with Ruby." He smiled.

"Thanks, Elijah."

"You're welcome. I'll see you tomorrow."

Just as I climbed out of the cab, I saw Nathan run up to the building.

"Hey," he said as he opened the door. "You're home early." He was nearly breathless.

"I just got out of court and Elijah told me to just come straight home."

"That was nice of him," he said as we approached the elevator and he pressed the button.

As soon as the doors opened and the people inside the elevator stepped out, we walked in and I pushed the buttons to both our floors.

"Are you going to Elijah's party tomorrow night?" he asked to make small talk.

"Yeah. I'll be there."

"Me too."

"So, I haven't seen you around the building all week."

"I was working all week. I'm off now for the next four days."

"Nice." I slowly nodded my head in awkwardness as I stared at the digital number up above wishing the elevator would move faster.

Suddenly, after we hit floor nine, the elevator jolted and came to a complete stop.

"What the fuck!" Nathan yelled. "This is the second time today. That's it, I'm moving out of this damn building."

Great. Just great. Seriously?

"It's always getting stuck between floors nine and ten. How many times does this have to happen before they do something about it?" he said. "Can we sue the building for this?"

"You can sue for negligent infliction of emotional distress, but you have to prove it."

"I am emotionally distressed. This is the second time today I've been stuck in here."

"You could sue for breach because the building isn't making the necessary repairs to ensure the elevator is fixed because it keeps breaking down."

"Good. Let's do it. I'm officially hiring you as my attorney." He smirked. "Since we're stuck here, maybe this is a good time to have our talk."

CHAPTER 47

*A*llison

My heart started racing. I wasn't ready to talk to him. Not here and not now. But I had a feeling I had no choice.

"Nathan, I honestly don't think there's anything to talk about."

He sat down on the ground with his back up against the wall.

"Have a seat." He patted the ground.

"Nathan—"

"Suit yourself if you want to stand in those heels for god knows how long."

I sighed as I sat down next to him.

"Fine. You want to talk. Talk."

"I'm sorry for what happened that night between us."

"I know. You've apologized already."

"Not properly because you wouldn't let me. Things are complicated with me in case you haven't already figured that out."

"Trust me. I figured it out. You know what?" I turned to him. "It really pissed me off how you blamed me for making you care." I raised my voice at him.

"That's because it's your fault. If you weren't such a damn amazing woman, I wouldn't have cared. But I do, and it's because I think you are the most incredible and sexy woman I've ever met. Hence the reason why it's your fault. You should be taking that as a compliment."

As much as I wanted to lash out at him, I couldn't. The only thing I could do was let a smile cross my lips.

"But seriously, Allison, I care about you in more ways than you'll ever know and hurting you was the biggest mistake of my life. If I could go back in time and rewrite that night, I would. I miss you and Ruby and I want the both of you back in my life."

I reached over and lightly took hold of his hand.

"I want you to come back into our lives as our friend. That's all I can give you and I hope you can understand that." I gave his hand a gentle squeeze. "I need you to understand."

"I do understand. Can you send me a nude selfie?"

"What?" I laughed as I smacked his arm. "No."

"Why? I'm not having sex with anyone else, so I'll need your picture for when I—you know." The corners of his mouth curved upward.

The elevator started moving and we both got up.

"I can't believe you just said that."

"Why? It's the truth."

The elevator stopped on the twenty-second floor and as soon as the doors opened, I stepped out and shook my head at him with a smile.

"Oh come on, Allison. You totally can believe I said that." He winked as a smile crossed his lips.

I stepped inside my apartment and Ruby came running over to me.

"Mom, you're home."

"I would have been home sooner, but the damn elevator got stuck."

"Me and Nathan got stuck in it earlier."

"What? You were stuck in the elevator with Nathan?"

"Yeah. We had a long talk. We're friends again. He painted a picture with me in the art room before he went for his run."

"Mom, can you stay with her for a little bit longer, I have to go have a chat with Nathan?"

"Of course. Go ahead and take your time." She smiled.

I went to the elevator and pushed the button. Then I decided to take the stairs three flights up instead. Knocking on his door, he answered it shirtless and in nothing but his running shorts. I swallowed hard as his six-pack stared me in the face.

"Allison?"

"Why didn't you tell me you were stuck in the elevator earlier with Ruby?" I pushed past him.

"I told you it was the second time today it happened."

"But you left out the fact that it was with my daughter," I shouted.

"I didn't really have a chance because we had started our conversation about that night."

"Can you please go put on a shirt."

"Why?" He smiled. "Am I making you uncomfortable?"

"No. It's just—"

"Just what?" He walked over to me and placed his hands on my hips.

"Stop it, Nathan," I said as I turned away from him and his arms wrapped around me.

My skin was trembling and all I could feel was the pulsating down below. The bad thing was I didn't try to get away from him like I should have.

"Have I ever told you how sexy you are when you're angry?" he whispered in my ear.

I swallowed hard as I could feel his cock pressing into my back. Don't do it, Allison. Don't do it. Screw it.

I turned around and smashed my mouth into his. Our kiss was wild and passionate, and I missed it. His fingers undid the button of my suitcoat as he slid it off my shoulders and let it drop to the floor.

"We don't have a lot of time. I told my mom I'd be right back."

"We don't need a lot of time, love. In fact, we're not even going to make it into the bedroom."

As I kicked off my shoes, I pulled my cami over my head while he unzipped my skirt and pulled it off my hips along with my panties. I pulled down his shorts and took his hard cock in my hand, giving it a few strokes as light moans escaped him.

"We have to stop for a minute. I need to go get a condom."

"No. Don't stop. I'm on birth control so you don't have to worry."

"Are you sure?" he asked in between kisses.

"Yes. Now fuck me."

He picked me up as my legs wrapped around his waist and my arms wrapped tightly around his neck. Carrying me to the wall, he set my back against it and thrust into me, inch by inch until he was buried deep inside. I gasped at the pleasure that overtook me. His tongue slid across my neck as the speed of his thrusting increased. My nails dug into his back as my body tightened and an orgasm washed over me.

"That's it, love. Yes. Yes. Oh my God." He slowed his pace and strained as he filled me up inside.

He looked at me, trying to regain his breath with a smile on his face.

"This never happened," I said.

"No. It never happened." He brushed his lips against mine.

He put me down and I quickly got dressed.

"I'll see you tomorrow at the party," I spoke as I headed towards the door.

"Wait a second," he said as he walked over to me and ran his hand down the back of my hair. "You had a little bit of sex hair." He grinned.

"Oh. Thanks." I bit down on my bottom lip before walking out the door.

I was lying in bed doing some work when my phone dinged with a text message from Nathan.

"You know that thing that didn't happen earlier?"

"Yeah."

"I can't stop thinking about it. It was amazing even though it never happened."

I let out a light laugh.

"Yeah. It was pretty amazing for never happening."

"Goodnight, Allison."

"Goodnight, Nathan."

The next day, after I dropped Ruby off at my parents' house, I headed to Aspen's and Elijah's. When I walked in, people were scattered everywhere, and waiters walked around holding up trays with appetizers on them.

"Yay. You're here." Aspen smiled as she ran up to me and grabbed my hand.

"Happy Birthday, Elijah." I kissed his cheek.

"Thank you, and thanks for coming. Can I get you a drink?"

"I'll go get one. Don't worry," I said as I looked around for Nathan.

I saw Mason at the bar, so I walked over.

"Hi, Mason."

"Hey, Allison. You look fantastic."

"Thanks. Is Nathan here yet?"

"Yeah. He's upstairs with Mila. She was screaming her head off and the nanny couldn't seem to calm her down, so Nathan went up there. It's weird how that kid naturally stops crying when she sees him."

"Will you excuse me for a moment?" I placed my hand on his arm.

"Of course."

I took the back stairs off the kitchen and headed up to the second floor. The door to Mila's room was half open, and when I peeked inside, I saw Nathan holding her and singing Here Comes The Sun in the rocking chair. I couldn't help but smile as I quietly stood there and watched for a moment. She was finally asleep and when he went to get up and put her in her crib, I quickly made my way back downstairs and over to the bar.

"What can I get you?"

"I'll have a whiskey sour, please."

"Well, well. A girl after my own heart," I heard Nathan's voice from behind. "Hello there, beautiful friend."

"Hey there, friend." I smiled.

"How long have you been here?"

"Not long. I wondered where you were."

"I was upstairs trying to get Mila to go to sleep. She was having a little hissy fit and I can calm her down."

"It must be all that charm you possess." I smirked.

"It must be. The child has good taste." He gave me a wink. "You look beautiful. In a friend way of course."

CHAPTER 48

Nathan

"Thank you, friend." She smiled.

"I'll have a scotch," I spoke to the bartender.

He handed me my drink and I held it up to Allison.

"To friendship."

"To friendship." She clanked her glass against mine.

"I'm going to go and talk to Colleen and Marie," Allison said.

"Of course. I have people over there I need to speak with. I'll talk to you later."

"Sure." The corners of her mouth curved upward.

I walked away and headed over to where Mason and Elijah stood.

"What was going on over there? Elijah asked.

"Nothing. We were just talking."

"So you're on speaking terms again?" Mason asked.

"Yeah. We got stuck in the elevator together yesterday. I was actually thinking about suing the damn building, but I was grateful because she had no choice but to listen to me."

"So the two of you talked?" Elijah asked.

"We did, and we decided just to be friends."

"And you're okay with that?" he asked.

"I'm totally fine with it." I smirked as I stared at Allison's ass in her short black dress while she stood and talked to Marie and Colleen.

After talking with my brothers and a few friends of mine, I walked over to Allison and whispered in her ear.

"That thing that never happened yesterday could never happen again if you would like to meet me in the bathroom upstairs."

"Are you serious? We can't do that?"

"Sure we can." I smiled as I walked away and headed upstairs.

A moment later, as I stood there, leaning up against the counter, Allison stopped in the doorway. Holding out my hand, she placed hers in mine and I pulled her inside, shutting and locking the door behind her. I placed my hand up her dress and pulled down her panties, feeling the wetness that emerged from her as I plunged a finger inside. She gasped as her fingers fumbled with the button on my pants. Lifting her on the counter, I thrust inside her, taking in the pleasure and the warmth that enveloped my cock.

When we were finished, I pulled up my pants, grabbed her panties and slid them on her.

"You better go out first. I'm going to clean up the evidence." I grinned as I kissed her lips.

"Okay. I'll see you downstairs. Remember, this never happened."

"It totally never happened."

I cleaned up the tissues and flushed them down the toilet. Walking out of the bathroom, I saw Elijah standing down the hallway with his arms folded and a displeased look on his face.

"Did you and Allison just have sex in my bathroom?"

"We sure did, bro. We sure did." I smiled and patted his shoulder as I walked by.

❧

The party was ending, and I asked Allison if she wanted to share a cab home. She agreed, so we said our goodbyes and left.

"That was a great party, don't you think?" she asked.

"It was a great party and I'm not even drunk." I gave her a smirk.

The cab pulled up to the building and we both climbed out. The elevator stopped on her floor, and when the doors opened, she grabbed my hand and led me out behind her.

"What are you doing?"

"Taking you home with me." She turned her head and gave me a smile. "But this never happened."

"No. Of course not." I grinned.

We had sex again. Wild and crazy sex to be exact. Damn. It felt like my cock was going to fall off, but I wasn't complaining. It felt good to hold her in my arms again and after the events of yesterday and today, I had to have another talk with her.

"I can't do this again, Allison."

"What?" She lifted her head and looked at me.

"I can't have sex with you anymore unless we are—well, you know, are—" I struggled with the words.

"A couple?"

"Yes, that." He pointed his finger at me.

"You won't have sex with me unless we're a couple? Is that a threat, Nathan Wolfe?"

"Actually it is a threat, love. You don't think I'm just giving this out for nothing, do you? Absolutely not. If you want this," I placed my hand on my cock, "then it comes with a price. It comes with sleepovers, family gatherings, dates, games, dancing and singing in the living room, stupid fights and whatever else couples do. It also comes with the words 'I love you' every day. That's the only way you'll get more of this. I'm not running a free shop here."

"Oh my God." She busted out into laughter. "You're such an asshole."

"I know I am, and you love it."

The smile that was on her face dissipated as she turned serious.

"I don't know if I'm a hundred percent ready."

"Listen, love, me either. But how are we going to know unless we give it a try. I don't want you to feel guilty about us because of Jared, and I never want you to stop talking about him. I want to hear all about the good times you had and how happy he made you. I want those memories to stay with you forever, but I also want you to have new memories of us. Ones we make together, as a couple."

"Nathan—"

I brought my thumb up and placed it on her chin.

"I love you, Allison. I'm madly in love with you and I want more. I'm all in, love, and I'm hoping you will be too."

"I love you too, Nathan, and I'm all in. Let's do this crazy little thing called life together."

"Couldn't have said it better myself." I rolled her on her back and hovered over her naked body as I kissed her lips. "Now you may have this whenever you desire." I smirked as I pushed myself inside her.

CHAPTER 49

*A*llison

Damn it. His charm was way too much to handle and I didn't even get a chance to make him work for my love. Oh well, he earned it, and I was more than happy to give it to him. He was hard to resist, and I knew I was going to have my hands full with the women who were going to ogle him every time we went out.

The next morning, after we had breakfast, Nathan went up to his apartment to shower and change before coming back down so we could have a talk with Ruby when she got home. Then there was telling my parents and Rick about us, not to mention Jared's parents that made me nervous as hell.

My Dad dropped Ruby off while my mom stayed home to prep for some luncheon she was having tomorrow.

"Hey, Mom," Ruby spoke as she walked through the door.

"Hey, sweetheart. Did you have fun with Grandma and Grandpa?"

"Yep. We had a lot of fun. Grandpa taught me how to golf."

"Wow. Hey, Dad." I smiled as I kissed his cheek. "Ruby, take your bag to your room and unpack it, please."

"Hey, baby girl. I have to get going. I need to help your mom out."

"Thanks for dropping Ruby off."

"No problem. How about dinner Tuesday night? We can go to that Italian place you love so much."

"Sounds good. Would you mind if I brought someone?" I bit down on my bottom lip.

"A man?" His brow arched.

"Yeah."

"Nathan Wolfe?"

"Maybe." I smiled.

"Of course you can bring him. Is there something you need to tell us?"

"Don't say anything to Mom because I want to tell her, but we're dating. Ruby doesn't know yet. He's coming over soon and we're going to tell her."

"She'll be thrilled. I know how much she likes him. I'm happy for you sweetheart. I knew you'd know when the right time was."

Ruby came running from her room, turned on the TV and plopped herself down on the couch. After my father left, I sent a text message to Nathan.

"My dad just dropped Ruby off."

"I'm on my way down. I love you."

"I love you too."

A few moments later, there was a knock at the door.

"Ruby, can you see who's at the door?"

"Sure, Mom. Nathan!" I heard her exclaim.

"Hey there, kiddo. How are you?"

"I'm good. What are you doing here?"

"I came over to see you," he said.

"Hey, Ruby, go sit down on the couch. Nathan and I want to have a talk with you."

"If you're not going to tell me you're dating, I don't want to hear it."

I looked at Nathan who had the same surprised look on his face as I did.

"We are dating," I said.

"Yay! That was fast. Does this mean Nathan's always going to be around?"

"It does, kid. I'm going to be around a lot."

"Good." She smiled.

"Ruby, there's something else I want to talk to you about."

"What is it, Mom?"

Shit. I didn't know how to come out and say it.

"Well—"

"What your mom is trying to say is that I'm going to spend the night here sometimes, if that's okay with you?"

Ruby's eyes widened.

"That's okay with me. I think it'll be fun to have sleepovers. But just keep it down while I'm sleeping, okay?"

"Now that I can't promise you, kid," Nathan spoke, and I smacked his arm.

"Are you sure, Ruby?"

"Yes, Mom. I'm sure. I'm happy you two made up." She hugged us both.

CHAPTER 50

SIX MONTHS LATER

*N*athan
Life was great. The only complaint I had was when I had to work long stretches and leave Allison and Ruby. For the most part, I cut way back on doing international flights because I wanted to be home more. A few of the other captains had retired and I was moving up which allowed me to pick more of the flights I wanted to fly. Ones that got me home at a decent hour.

When Allison worked and I was off, I picked Ruby up from school. She was a great kid and so far, she hadn't given us any trouble. I felt like an instant dad and the thing was, I liked it. Her guitar skills were improving. Especially since I bought her one of her own. She was getting so good at it that we were able to play together.

I stepped through the door at 40 Sullivan Street in Soho and looked at my watch. My brothers would be arriving any minute and I couldn't wait to get their opinion.

"Why are we here?" Elijah asked as he and Mason stepped inside.

"Welcome to Casa Wolfe." I held out my hands with a smile.

"What?" Mason said.

"You bought this place?" Elijah asked.

"Not yet. But I'm hoping to. I need to get Allison's opinion first.

I'm taking our relationship to the next level and asking her and Ruby to move in with me. Our apartments are just too small for the three of us."

"Damn, bro. You're moving fast." Mason smiled.

"He's doing just fine." Elijah grinned as he placed his hand on my shoulder.

I took them on a tour and they both loved it.

"You do realize you're really close to Mom, right?" Elijah asked.

"Yeah. Like just around the block," Mason said.

"I know." I sighed. "But this place is a steal right now. It's in foreclosure and the price is too good to pass up."

"Excuse me, Mr. Wolfe." Nancy, the realtor stepped inside the house. "I just wanted you to know that someone put down a deposit on this place."

"What? When?"

"About an hour ago. My partner who listed the house just called me."

"Shit." I shook my head.

"He told the interested party that they have twenty-four hours to make a final decision and to get the paperwork started if they want it. I'll call you if they change their mind. In the meantime, I can show you something else."

"No need, Nancy. I wanted this place. Shit."

"Don't worry, Nathan. Maybe they'll change their mind," Elijah said.

"Why would they at this price?"

*A*fter I picked Ruby up from school, I heard my phone ding with a text message from Allison.

"*My mom is coming over to get Ruby and take her to dinner. Want to go out tonight?*"

"Want to stay home and have wild and crazy sex instead?" I replied.

"*Yes, but I want to take you somewhere. It's a surprise.*"

"I love your surprises. I'm in. What time are you going to be home?"

"In about an hour. Be ready. I love you."

"I love you too."

What surprise did she have for me? Ah, I knew what it was. She was taking me to that new Mediterranean place I've been wanting to try for the last couple weeks. She must have got us a reservation.

After Carol came to pick up Ruby, I put on my shoes and made sure I was ready for when Allison got home. I heard my phone ding in my pocket, and when I pulled it out, there was a text message from Allison.

"I'm down in the cab. Get your hot ass out here."

"You're not even going to come up first?"

"No. I told you to be ready. Now hurry up and don't take the elevator in case you get stuck again."

"You want me to go down twenty-two flights of stairs?"

"Going down is the easy part. So yes, hurry up."

What the hell was going on with her? I was a nervous wreck as I stood in the elevator. There was no way I was going down twenty-two flights of stairs. I let out a deep breath when the elevator reached the lobby. Sliding next to her in the cab, I smiled as I kissed her lips.

"Hi."

"You didn't take the stairs, did you?"

"No."

She opened her briefcase and took out a blindfold.

"Put this on." She handed it to me.

"Wow. Aren't you a kinky little kitten." I grinned.

"Just put it on. I don't want you to see where I'm taking you just yet."

I was so confused as to what was going on. This wasn't like her, but I wasn't going to lie and say I didn't like it. In fact, it turned me on. I felt the cab pull away from the curb as I grabbed onto her hand. When the cab stopped, I started to take off the blindfold and she stopped me.

"No. Not yet."

"Allison, what is going on? We're here, aren't we?"

"Yes. But I can't let you take it off yet."

"Then how the hell am I supposed to see?"

"You're going to let me guide you."

I sighed as she helped me out of the cab and led me a few feet down the street.

"There are three steps going up. Don't trip."

"I'll try my best, but to be honest, this is scaring me."

"Stop being a baby."

I heard a door open and she guided me inside. Where the hell had she taken me? It was completely silent, and I knew we weren't at a restaurant.

"Okay. Now you can look," she said as she took off the blindfold.

I was in total shock as I stood in the same foyer that I was in earlier today with Elijah and Mason.

"Allison, what—"

"What do you think?"

"Mr. Wolfe?" Nancy cocked her head as she walked in from the other room.

"Do you two know each other?" Allison asked me.

"Wait, I'm confused," Nancy spoke.

"Is this the person who put down a deposit today?" I asked Nancy.

"Yes."

"Nathan. What's going on?" Allison asked with concern.

"I can't believe this. I fucking can't believe this." I grinned. "Baby, this is blowing my mind. I want this house. I was looking at it and fell in love with it and I wanted to bring you by to see it first, but Nancy told me that someone put down a deposit already."

"Shut up! So you already saw this house?"

"Yes. I fell in love with it the moment I saw it. Especially the—"

"Rooftop terrace with the outdoor kitchen and fireplace," we both said at the same time.

"Yes! Oh my God, Nathan." She threw her arms around my neck.

"But wait. Why were you looking at houses?" I asked her.

"Because I feel like the apartment is too small for the three of us. I was going to ask you how you felt about moving in together. Then I found this, and the price was too good to pass up. So I put down a deposit so no one else could steal it until I showed you."

"I felt the same way and I was going to put down a deposit so I could show it to you. Love of my life, will you do me the honor of moving into this beautiful house with me where we can make beautiful memories together?"

"Yes!" She hugged me tight.

I looked over at Nancy who had tears in her eyes and gave her a thumbs up.

CHAPTER 51

TWO MONTHS LATER

*A*llison
It was moving day and I couldn't wait to move into my beautiful new home with Nathan and Ruby. Nathan didn't have to worry about his lease because he rented month to month. I, on the other hand had about three months left on mine. Being the lawyer I was, I negotiated with the building manager because of the issue with the elevator that occasionally still got stuck between floors nine and ten. I was only held to pay one more month of rent which was fine with me.

"I love this place so much!" Ruby exclaimed as she ran around the six thousand seven hundred square foot home."

"No running!" I shouted as she was out of ear reach.

"Hello, hello," I heard Caitlin's voice.

"Great. Now she can just pop by at any time." Nathan rolled his eyes. "Hello, Mother." He kissed her cheek.

"Hi, Caitlin." I smiled.

"I just dropped by to give you a housewarming gift." She grinned as she handed us a white envelope.

Nathan opened it and we both looked at it in shock. It was a sizable gift certificate to the furniture store where we had been looking at furniture.

"Mom, we can't accept this."

"Don't be silly. Neither one of you have enough furniture to furnish this entire place, and I know you were waiting until you moved in. So, I thought that was the perfect housewarming gift."

"Thank you, Caitlin." I hugged her.

"Thanks, Mom. That was very generous of you."

Later that night, after we put Ruby to bed, Nathan and I cuddled on the couch in the living area amongst all the boxes that surrounded us.

"This is perfect," we both said at the same time.

"You know what would even be more perfect?" he asked.

"What?"

"If you'd marry me."

"What?" I lifted my head and looked at him in shock.

He reached in his pocket and pulled out a small velvet box and flipped open the lid.

"I love you, Allison. Maybe this is too soon. Who the hell knows. All I know is I want to spend the rest of my life with you and only you."

"I love you too, Nathan. And yes, I will marry you," I spoke as tears filled my eyes.

He took the 2-carat white gold, princess cut ring from the box and slipped it on my finger. Perfect fit. Do you like it it? Because if you don't, we can exchange it."

"I love it. It's perfect." I kissed his lips. "You have amazing taste, Mr. Wolfe," I said as I held out my finger.

"Did she say yes?" I heard Ruby ask from the stairs.

"She said yes, kid." Nathan smiled.

"Yay!" She ran down the stairs and jumped on our laps. "Congratulations, Mom."

"You knew about this?" I tickled her.

"Yes. Who do you think helped Nathan pick out the ring?"

I looked at Nathan and he gave me a wink.

"So now that you're getting married, when can I have a brother or sister?"

"Time for bed," Nathan said as he got up, threw her over his shoulder and carried her upstairs.

"Goodnight, Ruby."

"Goodnight, Mom," she shouted.

Nathan

After I tucked Ruby in again, I walked down the stairs and passed the living room.

"Hey, where are you going?" she asked from the couch.

"I'll be there in a minute," I said as I went into the kitchen and stood at the sink.

"If you're getting a drink, can you—Nathan, what's wrong?"

"Nothing." I wiped my eyes as I turned on the water.

"You're lying." She walked over and lightly took hold of my arm. "Were you crying?"

"No. Don't be ridiculous. I have something in my eye."

"Both of them?" She arched her brow. "What's wrong? Are you regretting asking me to marry you?"

"Oh my God, baby, no." I grabbed her and held her tight.

"Then what's wrong?"

"Your daughter. That's what's wrong."

"What did she do?"

I broke our embrace and wiped the tear that fell from my eye.

"She called me Dad."

She stood there in shock as she placed her hand over her mouth.

"If you don't want her calling you—"

"No. I do. That's the point. It made me so happy to hear that. These stupid things are uncontrollable happy tears."

"Aw, Nathan." She hugged me as she laughed.

"It's not funny, Allison."

"Yes, it is. What would your brothers say if they knew?"

I broke our embrace and narrowed my eye at her.

"You're not going to tell them. Not one word about what you just saw to anyone. Understand me?"

"Roar. You're sexy when you're crying and being authoritative." She grinned as she ran out of the kitchen.

"I mean it, love, you better not breath a word of this to my brothers!" I chased after her up the stairs.

※

A couple days later, we went to family dinner at my mother's house. We had already told Allison's family about our engagement last night and tonight it was our turn to tell my family. After we ate dinner, we all gathered in the living room like we always did, and I grabbed my glass of scotch to make a toast.

"I would like to make a toast," I held up my glass of scotch and took hold of Allison's hand.

Everyone picked up their glasses and held them up.

"I asked Allison to marry me and she said yes!" I grinned.

"Oh my God!" Aspen exclaimed as she hugged us both. "This is so exciting."

"Congratulations, darling." My mother smiled as she hugged me and then turned her attention to Allison. "I am so happy to have you as my daughter-in-law." She hugged her.

"Congratulations, brother." Elijah hugged me. "I'm so proud of you.

"Congrats, bro," Mason said. "I knew you'd cave." He hugged me. "And Mom better not get any ideas about me getting me married. Because it isn't happening."

"We'll see, little brother." Elijah smiled.

I felt a tugging on my pant leg and when I looked down, Mila stood there with her arms held up to me.

"Up. Up."

I bent down and picked her up.

"Hey there, sweet girl."

She giggled as she pulled my nose.

"Any talk about babies yet?" Elijah asked.

"Nah, not yet. Someday we'll have that talk."

"From what I can see between Mila and Ruby, you're going to make a great dad."

"Only because I learned from the best, bro."

He smiled as he hooked his arm around me.

This was my life now. I had a job I loved, a great family and a beautiful fiancée and future daughter whom I loved very much. I thought I was happy before, jet-setting across the world, when actually I was just running from the one thing I feared the most: falling in love. My name is Nathan Wolfe, and this was my story of how one woman and her little girl changed the course of my entire life and changed me into the man I was proud to become.

THE RING

CHAPTER 1

Adalyn

It all started when I found a beautiful diamond ring nestled between two pieces of coral while scuba diving in Antigua with my boyfriend of three years, Stephen. It was our dream vacation, and we'd been saving a whole year for it. The white sandy beaches, the calming site of the clear turquoise blue waters, and the sunsets were just part of the amazing experience we had. We did everything we could during our time there which included a buggy tour to see the rural areas of the island, zip lining, snorkeling, swimming with the stingrays and finally scuba diving. Little did I know that two weeks after our perfect vacation, my life would completely do a one eighty and go to total shit.

You're probably wondering what the hell happened. Well, let me enlighten you. It was my birthday when I came home after being fired from my job to find Stephen packing his bags. He delivered the news that he'd met another woman when we returned from Antigua and he couldn't explain what he felt when he met her. So, after a lot of screaming and throwing things, he took his bags and walked out on me, our three-year relationship, and our Seattle apartment. In one day, and on my birthday none the less, my boss fired me, and my boyfriend broke up with me. Both events completely devastated me, and I thought my life was over. I barely got out of bed for a week, and the one day I did, it was because my best friend Carly dragged me out of the apartment and to lunch with her, I came home to find that my building had caught on fire and burnt to the ground. Thank God nobody was seriously hurt, but I lost everything I owned.

 I moved in with Carly and her husband of two years, Daniel, until I figured out what I was going to do. It seemed the best option for me was to go back home to California. That's where I was originally from, born and raised. I graduated from the University of Washington with a Master of Design degree while Carly graduated with an MBA. California was our home, and the plan was to attend the University of Washington together, graduate, and move back home. We were best friends like that who did everything together. Then she met Daniel a few months before we graduated, and it was insta love. In the meantime, I secured an intern position with a company called K&L Design Group, and they offered me a full-time position when I graduated. I liked Seattle; I liked my job and Carly was staying, so I stayed. Then I met Stephen, who gave me even more reason never to leave Seattle.

"Hey, you," Carly softly spoke as she sat down next to me on the bed. "Whatcha doing?"

"Thinking about how much my life sucks."

"Don't say that, Adalyn. You could have been home and injured or even killed when that fire broke out."

"Just my luck that I wasn't." I rolled my eyes.

"But you would have been if I hadn't dragged you out to lunch. Listen, I know things are rough, but you will get through it." She placed her hand on top of mine.

"I've decided to go back to California."

"As in move there?" she asked, and I could sense the worry in her voice.

"I don't know. Maybe. All I know is I need to get out of Seattle."

"I totally get that. I really do. But Seattle is your home and has been for the last twelve years. It was your home way before your job with K&L Designs and it was your home before Stephen. Don't let a couple bad things that happened here make you run away. Just give it more thought. I know you'll find another job soon and I'll help you find a new apartment. I hate to say this, Ad, but you could totally put a positive spin on the whole apartment fire thing."

"Seriously?" I glared at her.

"Yeah. That was a place you and Stephen got together. Maybe it's best that it happened so you can start fresh somewhere else. Somewhere where you don't have to be reminded of him."

What she said made a little sense, but I couldn't find a positive with the fact that all my belongings were burnt to ashes.

"Just think about it for a while." She squeezed my hand. "Grandma Lori is coming over for dinner and you're joining us."

"I really don't feel—"

"I said you're joining us. Besides, you know how Daniel is when it comes to his grandma. You really don't have a choice." A smirk crossed her lips.

"Then I guess I better get in the shower," I sighed.

I loved Grandma Lori. I'd known her ever since Carly and Daniel first got together. She was one of those cool hippy grandmas. She wore her gray hair long and curly and she always wore stylish hippy clothing with a lot of jewelry. She was a Theology professor at Seattle University and her wisdom and knowledge about everything always amazed me. She was a traveler who had lovers in just about every country she visited, but she could never bring herself to settle down with one special person.

We were all sitting at the table having dinner and listening to her latest adventures in Peru when she glanced over at me with a sympathetic look.

"I'm so sorry to hear about everything you're going through," she spoke.

"Thanks, Lori. It's been a tough few weeks." I looked down.

She reached over, placed her hand on mine and gave it a gentle squeeze.

"You'll get through it. What a beautiful ring," she spoke as she held up my hand and examined it. "That looks like it cost a fortune."

"Thank you. I found it scuba diving in Antigua. It was in between two pieces of coral. Look." I took it off. "It has an inscription on the inside."

To my darling Mary, my soulmate for life.

She read the inscription and then stared at me with the strangest look on her face.

"You found this when you were in Antigua you say?"

"Yeah. I found it on our last day there."

"Adalyn, listen to me carefully. You need to get rid of this ring."

"Why?" My brows furrowed.

"Honey, this ring is the reason everything bad has happened to you since you found it."

"Grandma Lori, that's ridiculous," Carly spoke.

"You have to listen to me, Adalyn. There are stories about this, and I've heard of it happening before. This ring is a symbol of true love. It was given to Mary by her soulmate to seal that love forever. It's not meant to be worn by anyone else. You must get rid of it immediately and as far away from you as possible. I don't mean to scare you, darling. Just do yourself a favor and dispose of it."

"You could always pawn it and get a shitload of money for it," Daniel said.

"No." Lori shot him a look. "Do you want the same awful things to happen to someone else? The ring must be disposed of or given back to its owner. Once it is out of your possession, it will break the curse."

"Curse?" I furrowed my brows.

"Yes, Adalyn. You should dispose of that ring immediately or bad things will continue to happen to you."

After Grandma Lori left, I grabbed a glass a wine and took it into my bedroom. As I was laying across the bed and sipping my drink, I held the beautiful white gold, diamond encased band in my hand and stared at it. As ridiculous and absurd as it sounded, I was thinking what Lori said was true. Ever since I returned from Antigua it had been one horrific thing after another. After finishing my wine, I set it down on the nightstand and grabbed my laptop. I would see if there was any truth to what Lori said. Stephen, my job and my apartment burning down weren't the only bad things that happened to me. Those were just the major ones. They declined my credit card at the department store when I was buying some new clothes. Apparently, someone had stolen my numbers and charged over five thousand dollars' worth of electronics. I knew that always happened to many people, but it had never happened to me. Then, I dropped my phone in the street and as I went down to pick it up, someone on a bike ran over it, forcing me to buy a new one. If that wasn't all, I came down with a sinus infection and prescribed some medication. The pharmacy gave me the wrong one, and I ended up having an allergic reaction and landed in the ER.

The next morning, I was up at the crack of dawn for I couldn't sleep. My mind had been racing with thoughts all night about that ring. Grandma Lori said I needed to get rid of it immediately and I would do just that. As I was studying the ring last night and the inscription, I had an idea, and let me tell you, it probably wasn't the best idea I'd ever had, but it was an idea so strong that I couldn't ignore it.

"Good morning." Carly smiled as she emerged into the kitchen and poured herself a cup of coffee. "I've decided that today is the day you will get your life back," she said as she leaned over the island where I was sitting. "No more moping around or feeling sorry for yourself. You will start by getting rid of that ring. I'm taking a half day from work, and we're taking the ferry to Bainbridge Island to do some shopping. While we're on the ferry, you will throw that ring into the Sound and forget you ever found it."

"That sounds like a great plan and as much as I'd love to, I can't."

"What?" Her brows furrowed.

"I'm going to New York. I booked a flight last night. It leaves in four hours."

She held her coffee cup between her hands and cocked her head at me as a look of confusion swept across her face.

"What do you mean you're going to New York?"

"On the inside of the ring is the name of the designer who designed it. It just so happens that he owns a custom jewelry shop in New York. I'm hoping that maybe he has records or something that will lead me to Mary. Then I can give her ring back to her and all will be right in the world and hopefully my life."

"That's the dumbest idea I've ever heard, Adalyn. First, you don't even know when that ring was lost or even if it was lost. For all we know something could have happened between Mary and her husband and she got rid of it on purpose. She may not want it back. Second, Mary could be anywhere in the world. Just because it was designed in New York doesn't mean shit."

"I guess I'll find out when I get there. But New York is the starting point. I have to try. If it doesn't pan out, I'll get rid of the ring while I'm there. I have to go pack," I said as I refilled my coffee cup and went into the bedroom.

"Hope you have no more bad luck on your little adventure," she shouted.

CHAPTER 2

Harrison

"Really, Harrison?" my sister, Athena, shouted as she stormed into my office.

Reaching into my desk drawer, I took out the bottle of aspirin and popped two of them in my mouth.

"Good morning, sis. Welcome home. How was Europe?" I asked with a smirk for I already knew why she blew in with an attitude.

"Renee was the best personal assistant I ever had, and you have to ruin her like all the other women in your life. I leave you alone for one month and you can't behave yourself or keep your dick in your pants."

"Calm down. Renee was the only personal assistant you ever had so don't say she's the best. It was one drunken night, Athena. One." I held up my finger. "It's not my fault she thought it would turn into something more. When I told her it was a mistake and it'll never happen again, she took it personally and quit. It's not my fault she's so sensitive."

"UGH! You can have any woman you want! I thought I made myself clear when I hired her that she was off limits!"

"Like I said, it was one drunken night. I didn't mean for it to happen. I'm sorry she couldn't handle it and quit. You'll find another assistant."

"That's not the point! I liked her." She pouted.

I got up from my chair, walked over to where she stood and wrapped my arms around her.

"I'm happy you're home. I missed you."

"I missed you too until I came back to no assistant." She broke our embrace.

"You'll get over it." I kissed her forehead and walked back to my desk.

"How are the plans for the townhouse coming?" she asked.

"I don't want to talk about it. At this rate, I'm never moving in."

"Why? What happened?" She took the seat across from my desk.

"Linda quit."

She let out a snicker. "Didn't she like work for you for a week?"

"Three days. I told her I didn't like what her plan was for the living room and I made her change it."

"Well, that's your right to do that. You're the client. I don't understand why she would quit over that. Unless you ran your mouth and insulted her." Her brow raised.

"All I said was she had terrible taste, and I didn't understand how she even got her degree."

Athena rolled her eyes and let out a sigh.

"Then maybe you need to decorate the townhouse yourself, brother. Obviously, no one can do it better than you."

"I don't have time for that. Do me a favor and find someone for me. Someone excellent who will take my criticism and not act like a child."

"Maybe if you were nicer, you could keep people around." She smirked. "Besides, I don't have time to find anyone for you. I just got back and now I have to find a new personal assistant." She got up from her chair and headed towards the door. "I'll be using your personal assistant, Jeremy, until I find one," she spoke as she walked out of my office.

I sighed as I leaned back in my chair and placed my hands behind my head. My twin sister could be such a pain in the ass. As I was pondering my thoughts about the townhouse, my phone beeped with a text message from Andrea.

"Hey there handsome, what time are you picking me up tonight?"

Shit. I forgot we were supposed to go on a date.

"How's seven o'clock?"

"Seven's good. If you want to bring me some flowers, yellow roses are my favorite."

I didn't reply. Why the hell would she want me to bring her flowers? I wasn't a flower giving type of guy. There were only two people in the world that I gave flowers to and that was my grandmother and Athena. I wasn't a romance type of guy either. As far as I was concerned, romance was overrated. There was no need for it. The women I took out got a nice dinner and then great sex afterwards. And usually the boot after a few dates because they started getting clingy and too attached. Something that I despised. There was nothing more pathetic than a woman whining and wanting to know why I wouldn't commit or take our so called 'relationship' to the next level. I didn't have time or the patience for that, and I didn't need the aggravation.

Now that Andrea had thrown in the 'flower' suggestion. I suspected it was time to cut all ties. I already knew how this would pan out. First it starts with the flowers, then the whining begins how I never want to do anything besides have dinner and sex. It got old real fast, and I cut my losses and move on. Which I had a feeling would happen tonight. Maybe I should just skip the dinner part and get right to the sex first before telling her we wouldn't be seeing each other anymore. I was under a great deal of stress with the building of the new hotel and I needed sex to get my mind off it.

Click the link below to download your copy of The Ring.
Amazon Universal Link:
mybook.to/TheRing

BOOKS BY SANDI LYNN

If you haven't already done so, please check out my other books. Escape from reality and into the world of romance. I'll take you on a journey of love, pain, heartache and happily ever afters.

Millionaires:

The Forever Series (Forever Black, Forever You, Forever Us, Being Julia, Collin, A Forever Christmas, A Forever Family)

Love, Lust & A Millionaire (Wyatt Brothers, Book 1)

Love, Lust & Liam (Wyatt Brothers, Book 2)

Lie Next To Me (A Millionaire's Love, Book 1)

When I Lie with You (A Millionaire's Love, Book 2)

Then You Happened (Happened Series, Book 1)

Then We Happened (Happened Series, Book 2)

His Proposed Deal

A Love Called Simon

The Seduction of Alex Parker

Something About Lorelei

One Night In London

The Exception

Corporate A$$ETS

A Beautiful Sight

The Negotiation

Defense

Playing The Millionaire

#Delete

Behind His Lies

Carter Grayson (Redemption Series, Book One)

Chase Calloway (Redemption Series, Book Two)

Jamieson Finn (Redemption Series, Book Three)

Damien Prescott (Redemption Series, Book Four)

The Interview: New York & Los Angeles Part 1

The Interview: New York & Los Angeles Part 2

One Night In Paris

Perfectly You

The Escort

The Ring

Elijah Wolfe

The Donor

Second Chance Love:

Rewind

Remembering You

She Writes Love

Love In Between (Love Series, Book 1)

The Upside of Love (Love Series, Book 2)

Sports:

Lightning

ABOUT THE AUTHOR

Sandi Lynn is a *New York Times, USA Today* and *Wall Street Journal* bestselling author who spends all her days writing. She published her first novel, *Forever Black*, in February 2013 and hasn't stopped writing since. Her mission is to provide readers with romance novels that will whisk them away to another world and from the daily grind of life – one book at a time.

Be a part of my tribe and make sure to sign up for my newsletter so you don't miss a Sandi Lynn book again!

Website

Newsletter

Bookbub

Pinterest

Goodreads

Printed in Great Britain
by Amazon